A VERY PROFITABLE WAR

A VERY PROFITABLE WAR

DIDIER DAENINCKX

TRANSLATED BY SARAH MARTIN

With Rémy and Ferdinand in mind

A VERY PROFITABLE WAR
First published in France as *Le der des ders* by Editions Gallimard, Paris

Translated by Sarah Martin

This edition published by arrangement with Serpent's Tail, London

First Melville House printing: December 2012

Melville House Publishing
145 Plymouth Street
Brooklyn, NY 11201

www.mhpbooks.com

ISBN: 978-1-61219-184-3

Manufactured in the United States of America
1 2 3 4 5 6 7 8 9 10

A catalog record for this book is available from the Library of Congress

CHAPTER 1

It all started at the beginning of January. It was cold as hell and I was knocking back hot toddies to keep me going through the day.

One part boiling water, three parts bourbon.

The tabloid I was reading had splashed the news of Deschanel's election as President of the Republic. Three years ago, between Craonne and Verdun, I had seen thousands of men mown down who could have done the job just as well; so you can imagine, I didn't give a shit for Deschanel.

But to come back to my story.

It must have been on the fifth. At least it was the first Monday of the month, and indeed of the year. I couldn't be mistaken: the Packard representative had just lifted 1500 francs off me.

A bit rough as a New Year's greeting! The worst of it was that he would do the same every month…

He was going to milk me again in February and March, then finish! I could climb behind the wheel of the Double-Six as sole and complete owner down to the last nut…

I had laid the table while Irène finished preparing the dinner. The smells wafting from the kitchen were full of promise. Things were simmering nicely.

What a bitter disappointment! I had barely swallowed my first mouthful before I pushed away my plate. The jelly-like mound in the middle, swimming in brown sauce, trembled for a few seconds before becoming still again.

'This is unbelievable! Did you mess it up or is it the ingredients?'

Irène looked at me, her eyes wide with surprise.

'Wait a minute, I'll have a taste.'

She cut a thin sliver of the moulded pâté she had decided on as the main dish. She raised the mouthful to her lips and spat it out instantly.

'Oh, you're right... How disgusting! It must come from the tin...'

'What tin? You're not going to tell me we're eating out of tins here?... Don't you think I've had my fill of tins? I got calluses on my thumb from using a tin-opener. Even they never dared to palm us off with junk as vile as this. Can you tell me what it is?'

'It's corned mutton. There's no need for such a song and dance. It's disgusting that's all. I'll throw away what's left.'

'Corned mutton... Where does that animal come from? I'd never heard of it before this meal!'

She shook her head, grimaced and raised her eyes to the ceiling, more than a touch exasperated.

'I suppose you've never heard of corned beef either then! Well, instead of using beef, they do it with mutton. They're selling off their stocks for next to nothing at the Vilgrain warehouses... You don't usually have a bad word for anything American.'

I leapt up. In two strides I was in the kitchen; the gaping tins sat like pisspots in the middle of yesterday's rubbish. I took one and deciphered the source of origin before coming back in triumph to the dining-room.

'They're not half-bad, your Americans! If you can read, have a look here. "Made in Scotland." Americans in kilts... that would be a sight. Take my advice: don't leap into international trading without at least some basic knowledge.'

She leant on the table edge to get up.

'I'll go and make something else.'

I was already leaning over her, making my intentions quite clear. Underneath the weight of brown hair, I was searching for the wine coloured mark behind her ear, the size and shape of a coffee bean; so desirable, like the one that decorated the inside of her thigh, high up.

You could become a fetishist over less.

Irène moved away. She settled herself on the bed, her gown wrapped around her, and looked at me tenderly.

'I'm not undressing, it's too cold in here.'

I was just about to join her when the telephone began to ring.

'Oh shit. They do it on purpose. That's the third time in less than a week.'

I put my trousers back on: I couldn't get into the habit of answering the phone half-naked, I felt as if the other person on the line could tell my state of undress by my tone of voice as I was talking.

Irène had none of these hang-ups; on the contrary, I think she took pleasure in it.

I unhooked the speaker and put it to my lips before reaching for the earphone.

'Is this the right number for the Griffon Agency?'

The voice was authoritative, sharp, and belonged to someone who didn't bother with small talk.

'Yes.'

'Could you put me through to René Griffon?'

Yet another who was used to domestic servants.

'Speaking. What's your problem?'

There was a short silence. It seemed as if he wasn't expecting me to take the initiative. It often happens like that. They take hours finally to decide to call me, going through all the questions and answers. Then, if you rushed things at the beginning, it would all fall apart. 'We haven't got to that point yet. I was hoping to use your services to sort out a little difficulty I'm having.'

'I'll be happy to help you. Come by the agency...'

Irène was signalling desperately from the depths of the bed.

'... but not for an hour or two. I have to go out.'

'I would prefer that you came to see me, it's very difficult for me to go out. It's extremely urgent. General Hordant was kind enough to give me your number...'

I let myself be reeled in. As usual. I could hardly see myself refusing to give a helping hand to a war invalid! Too bad about the meal, and the dessert... We promised to catch up at dinner-time.

I went back up to the Place du Maroc to reach the Rue de Flandre. A convoy of about thirty canvas-covered Hotchkiss lorries was going through the Vertus goods yard. I kept my car in a little garage in the Passage des Anglais, in the corner of the quay on the Seine, near the Jewish cemetery. The mechanic maintained it out of pleasure. He couldn't get over taking on a Packard. He could have made a fortune by establishing a sight-seeing tour: half the district must have had a look at the twelve cylinders in V formation! On the day it was delivered, I was stupid enough to leave it in front of the block of flats overnight. Some little wiseacre could think of nothing better to do than nick the radiator cap as a souvenir.

The apprentice was holding the fort while the boss and his mechanics were having a bite to eat in a restaurant round the corner. He hadn't heard me coming, so he didn't stop his sales patter to a young lady all of fifteen years old.

'This motor is a real dream! You start in third at five km/h and you can get to 130 without even trying ... The Citroëns and Renaults are left standing ...'

The girl was behind the wheel, her hair tossed back, ready to take off like the wind.

I raked the ground with my feet to announce my presence.

'The session's over, kids! I'm off out.'

The little slip of a thing quickly pushed open the door and jumped out next to the apprentice, whose face was turning crimson.

'Do you know how to start a car like this?'

'No, well ... yes.'

'Well, go on then. Show us what you can do.'

The kid couldn't believe his ears. He hesitated for a split second then made up his mind and climbed on to the running board. He leant over the leather seat, made sure the car was in neutral, then opened up the petrol feed. He pumped the accelerator to prime the carburettor and got down again. He bent over in front of the car, got hold of the crank and, feet slightly apart, put everything he had into it. The mechanism didn't need all that effort; the bodywork vibrated imperceptibly while a wisp of bluish smoke trickled from the rear of the car.

'Open the gate. Tell your boss I'll be back before he closes up... If not, I'll come and get the key from his home.'

I stayed in second the whole length of the dock at La Villette. I changed up to cruising speed when I got to the bend where the canals of Saint-Denis and l'Ourcq meet. Despite the cold, the smoke and heavy stench of the fertilizer factories was blown over Paris by the wind from the north-east and mixed with the acrid discharge from the gasometer at La Chapelle.

It had had a strange effect on me, hearing General Hordant's name over the phone: I didn't want to have anything to do with these ex-pacifists who boasted their violent hatred of Germans at countless dinner parties as soon as war was declared and who never let an opportunity slip to polish up their medals or iron their flags. They could be sure of one thing, I wasn't prepared to fall in line with them just to chew the fat in front of the Monument to the Fallen. For months, my mail had been swollen with subscription forms to the Friends of Old Soldiers, to Associations for Survivors of the Trenches... there were as many as there were shells on the Chemin des Dames!

Irène decided to get a bigger dustbin. To be quite honest, I hadn't been completely passed over. On 18 June, five months before the end, they had managed to land me with a Croix de Guerre with honours!

We were cleaning up 'the pillboxes', German fortifications in reinforced concrete, packed close together and defended by groups of machine-gunners. It was bucketing down; we were living in holes carved out by enemy shells, which instantly filled with water. The choice was either to drown or to make a run for it without cover…

I did what all the others did, ran as fast as I could with a fixed bayonet. Just to have done with it. It would seem the men opposite us were even more fed up than we were. With one charge, the hill fell into our hands, while we were just trying to escape getting bogged down in the mud and bodies.

Next week, General Hordant was pinning his trinket on my clean tunic. France was proud of me, according to him. I wasn't nearly so ebullient as I thought of all the soldiers with missing limbs rotting on the barbed wire made by Krupp or De Wendel.

Most of my colleagues would have straight away put the title in capital letters on their visiting card.

'Detective Arsehole'
CROIX DE GUERRE WITH HONOUR

A good idea, as you would no longer have to prove anything, you could just reap the benefits of one inglorious moment in the life of a squaddie at the end of his tether. I suppose it's stupid; but I felt I had to start working with a clean slate.

Do you want to see my card?

René GRIFFON, private detective
By appointment only
15 Rue du Maroc Paris 19e
Metro Bd. de la Villette
Tel: VIL 32.12

I'd started off like all the others, proof of adultery, quickie divorces. I was certainly never short of work. Freed for a few years from their husbands' yoke, women had changed more in those four years than since the 1870 war! And that's without taking into account all the crises provoked by the amputations... How could you hold it against a young woman of twenty-five who, on seeing her champion polka dancer come back in a wheelchair, couldn't bring herself to play second fiddle and carried on dancing with a different partner? I had a stroke of genius one day in a doctor's waiting-room where I was reading one of his house journals. A journalist had just spent several months visiting institutions that took care of those badly wounded in the war. There was a short chapter on the unlucky ones who were left mad or amnesiac by the savage combat. One year after the armistice they were still counting up hundreds of unidentified ex-combatants.

The doctor must still be looking for me. And for his magazine!

In less than a week I had the necessary authorization from the military authorities, then I got in touch with local photographers all over the country, to build up a portrait gallery of this assembly of ghosts. The press had broadcast my initiative as an act of charity, complete with purple prose and strings. From one day to the next I found myself turned into a switchboard operator. Telephone calls one after the other. Hundreds of families began to hope again, fathers, mothers whose thoughts for months had turned more and more towards the unknown soldier...

And, amid this sea of sentimentality, there were dozens of women married to a missing soldier, who were ready to recognize the first nutter they saw, just, finally, to get a divorce. My favourite clients ... they were the ones who unknowingly clubbed together to present me with my Double-Six.

I left the abattoirs behind on my right, and approached the city wall flanked by the stronghold of La Villette. Teams of workers were busy taking out the cornerstones from the fortifications. They had already cleaned up the Clignancourt district where all kinds of multi-purpose barracks were being built. Clusters of men were having a break in a café made of wooden planks. As I passed by I made out a tune being played on the phonograph ... I bet it was 'Les Triolets'.

My fingers were beginning to freeze. I decided to open the hot air vent: you always got a bit of exhaust fumes as well but it did make it a few degrees warmer.

On the phone, the client had advised me to branch off before the airfield at Dugny Le-Bourget, and to cross Le Blanc-Mesnil. He lived near the station at Aulnay-sous-Bois, Rue Thomas and had introduced himself as Colonel Fantin of the 296th infantry regiment. They too had been really put through it. At least the few of them who had come back ... *L'Illustration* had put out a special supplement on the 296th, the most decorated regiment in the world! Without counting the little white crosses ... Surely he wanted to see my portrait collection; I had made sure to bring along my albums.

The red belt seemed to have all the worst that Paris had to offer: slums as far as the eye could see marked out by stinking muddy streets, with a scattering of factories with pointed roofs from which sprang up a multitude of chimneys in sombre brickwork.

I couldn't go through an area like this without identifying

with the grimy kids playing amid the heaps of smoking debris. That's where I came from: behind the railway cuttings. Thank you France!

The landscape improved as I got nearer to Aulnay. Market gardens surrounded the suburban villas of the property-owning class and the spacious houses of skilled workers. A sort of urbanized country scene.

Rue Thomas began after the level crossing. I managed to cross it at full speed just in front of a train leaking steam from every joint while sending out intermittent hoarse whistles. I stopped outside number 12, an imposing middle-class house on three floors well protected by a concrete wall topped by a railing with sharp points. The bell pull swung gently in the breeze and knocked repeatedly against a china plate.

M. Fantin de Larsaudière

I didn't even have a chance to use the bell. Someone must have been looking out for me impatiently, because a window opened on the ground floor, framing the outline of a man with narrow shoulders.

'Come in, M. Griffon. The gate is only pushed to. Park your car behind the house, under the porch. The streets aren't very safe.'

I followed his advice. This gave me a chance to take a glance round the property, the orchard, the winter garden and especially a magnificent 1915 25 h.p. pea-green Vauxhall. I'd have put my head on the chopping block if this wasn't one of those cars of the English High Command that we used to see shuttling between the Embassy and Montmartre. My client had the wherewithal to buy himself an aristocratic name; he seemed to have enough left over to bring his surroundings up to his civilian status.

Stepping on to the polished parquet floor in the hall where Colonel Fantin was waiting for me, I adjusted my fees according to the decor: 100 francs a day plus expenses.

I wasn't deceived by the outline glimpsed at the window. The colonel, who must have been coming up to sixty, was a small lean man with a bony face; he had put on his uniform, intending to impress me or to get a bargain rate from me by playing on my patriotic feelings. He was leaning against the wall, his legs hidden by a leather armchair. He moved suddenly to meet me. I had the same feeling I would have had if the photo of a young girl, placed on the piano, had suddenly smiled meltingly for my benefit. The colonel must have noticed my astonishment.

'You think that my story on the telephone that I couldn't get around was just an excuse? It's just that I'm looking after my daughter.'

I hate getting angry with my clients before I know how much they value my services.

'Now I'm here it doesn't matter.'

His mouth lifted slightly at the corners, then he shook his head. The topic was closed as far as we were both concerned.

'I'm not in the habit of entrusting my affairs to anyone else, police, the law or similar. Believe me, if I had been able to deal with this myself, I would never have called on you. I need therefore to assure myself of your absolute discretion. Above and beyond my person, it's the army itself that is under attack.'

The rate rose to 110 francs.

'Perhaps we should start at the beginning of your story. Is someone trying to harm you?'

'Without a doubt! There's no danger in attacking me . . . In a manner of speaking, I am the prisoner of my own legend. When you've been in command of the most valiant regiment in France and led the entire army in the march-past on the 11th November 1918, you cannot permit yourself the slightest lapse . . .'

'Have you got concrete proof of these attempts to intimidate you?'

'First of all there were threatening phone calls. I didn't want to take them seriously . . . These were followed by anonymous letters, like this one.'

He took out a sheet of paper and held it out to me.

There was just one line of text, typewritten:

'Pay up if you don't want to be exposed on every front page in the country.'

'They typed that on an Underwood. They're all over the place since they've been selling off the American stockpile. I won't get anything out of that. Did it come in the post?'

'No, somebody must have slipped it into the letterbox, without an envelope.'

'Fine. To sum up, you want me to lay my hands on the person or persons who are having a good time sending you these letters . . . And of course to find out what makes them think you'll give in to them. Who and why!'

'I would consider myself quite satisfied with your services if I only knew who. I'm afraid I know only too well the reason for this blackmail.'

'You'd save a lot of trouble if you took me into your confidence.'

'It's my wife . . . She's becoming more and more careless.'

The admission cost him dearly. It showed.

'She'd fallen into the habit of keeping company with other men, during my assignments... I didn't take any notice before.'

I could imagine the scene with no difficulty. It would be as if the newspapers headlined 'Clemenceau the cuckold' and published in detail the unhappy love life of the Tiger. I came down to 100 francs again; the colonel became as pathetic as the nice ladies who looked for a husband in my albums so they could get a speedy divorce and pocket a share of the nutcase's money!

'My condolences, colonel. I'll sort things out. It shouldn't take long... Has the blackmailer told you how much he wants?'

'He should be contacting me by phone this week. I'm waiting. You can take care of any money to be handed over should the necessity arise. The one essential thing in this affair is to avoid any publicity. I need to know who it is to make sure he isn't tempted to try again.'

'I don't need to know any more, Mr Fantin. My rate is 100 francs a day, not including expenses, of course. You can settle up when the job's done.'

Before leaving the room, I glanced one last time at the photo on the piano. It was only then I noticed the extraordinary resemblance to the colonel's face. Nothing to be ashamed of though; it was a pretty face with strongly marked features. The photographer had been able to capture an air of serious charm: a gaze filled with immense sadness.

'Someone in the family?'

'Yes, it's my daughter, Luce.'

As I left, I turned the first doorknob I came across and found myself looking into the toilets. Colonel Fantin blushed and waved me to the exit.

I got back to Paris without any hold-ups. Irène was waiting for me impatiently.

Before she slipped into bed, she took the phone off the hook.

CHAPTER 2

While the colonel touched his cap to democracy by calling himself plain Fantin, his wife did nothing of the sort. Mme de Larsaudière trailed her aristocratic name like a bait in every fashionable night-club in Montmartre.

I nursed a few contacts with some touts in cabarets on the Boulevard de Clichy. For a while they tried to reintegrate the war-wounded; doorman is not the hardest of jobs. But soon it was no longer fashionable to watch the parade of bodies ruined by the war. There is no pity. People came looking for love and kicks: the wide boys from the suburbs gathered on the pavement again.

This time round it was Bob, an American, who set me on the trail. He had chosen to stay in Paris after being demobbed; he spent his time divided half and half between the army surplus warehouse in Saint-Denis Pleyel and the dives in the 18th where English was spoken as much as slang, once night fell. He was a kind of guide, a streetwise operator, who lived off a percentage of every glass of wine and every meal swallowed by the groups of amazed tourists that he trundled from Pigalle to Blanche.

I took advantage of his generosity by taking a monthly trip round the warehouse at Pleyel. In 1917, the Yanks had set off for a ten-year war. They hadn't stinted on the Supply Corps; everything that more than a million men could want for their daily needs for months had been neatly piled up in a multitude of hangars scattered around French territory. Unfortunately it was all settled within a year! Jerry was trashed...

No question of wrapping up the tanks to send them home (the Indians had been KO'd for years) nor the mountains of French letters made in Ohio! The American women were clean, not like these French whores...

Once they sold off a complete railway, tracks, machines, engines, carriages, shunting mechanisms. Fifty kilometres of track between Boulogne-sur-Mer and Fauquembergues, in the Pas-de-Calais. To be dismantled.

I was more modest. I kitted myself out with small portable items and food: fruit juices, cakes, beer, Cokes. I paid for half the items. Bob dealt with the bills. Once he had managed to dig out two new tyres for the Packard. A windfall that came out of a swop with the English supplies. I phoned Pleyel without success: no one had seen him in his old haunts for a couple of days. I had no choice but to pace the streets.

I met him two days after my visit to Aulnay when he was packing about twenty young Australian women into the entrance hall of the Chamberlain studio, the photographer of the Médrano circus. Bob looked like Tom Mix without his hat. The gangling body of a disillusioned cowboy. He won the confidence of his future victims by means of a constant smile and of a surprising and hesitant slowness of gesture.

I pretended not to recognize him. He called me over.

'Hey René!'

I pretended to be surprised even though I'd been hanging

around for hours just to find him. 'Hi, Bob. I didn't expect to see you here. What's cooking?'

'I'm trailing some Australian widows around. They get their passage paid to France to do a tour of the military cemeteries but I reckon they're more interested in Pigalle. You should come by Pleyel, we've got some new stuff.'

He pinched the top of his trouser-leg and rubbed the rough blue material between thumb and index.

'Jeans (he drawled out the word). As many as you could get through in a life-time! Blue-jeans. Something for the bachelor boy. You don't have to iron them. By the way are you still stringing along your widows, like me?'

'No, I'm looking for some information on a high roller. A lady with a bit of class.'

'There's no shortage of that type around here. A jealous husband?'

'Oh, sure; it's kind of rare for a lover to be footing the bill for a detective. If by any chance you hear any rumours about her on your rounds, let me know. She's called Amélie Fantin …'

Bob shook his head.

'Doesn't ring any bells offhand … But I could put down a few markers …'

The photographer suddenly burst out of the doorway of his boutique, looking pretty irritated.

'Come quickly, Mr Bob. These women are insisting that they're taken alongside the Fratellinis … They claim that you promised them that …'

He favoured me with a friendly slap on the back.

'I'll leave you now. Business calls … No sweat. You'll see, we'll sort out this little problem.'

I believed him, he'd pulled himself out of far tighter corners before.

While I was out, Irène had dug out the Fantin family tree with a dozen phone calls. The secret is in the voice. With her latest model phone she got through as much work as a whole team of detectives! She threw herself at me as soon as I stepped into the flat.

'I can see why your colonel is so fond of his wife. She's the one who holds the purse strings.'

'Congratulations. How did you get to that?'

'It's not important... Fantin de Larsaudière comes from Charente. An old agricultural family settled near Cognac. Make no mistake, this is an authentic blue-blooded family. They've even been ruined.'

'In that case there can be absolutely no doubt about their title.'

'Exactly. They must be part of that aristocracy that refused to become industrialists like all the others. In Cognac the gossip about your colonel's marriage to Amélie Darsac is inexhaustible. That's the attraction of these little towns—it all comes spilling out!'

'Firstly, he's not my colonel, he's my client! Secondly, I'd like to know what you hinted at to make everyone tell you all these secrets without even knowing you.'

By way of an answer she just slowly licked her tongue over her lips, coating them with a glossy film. Message received.

'He who dares wins! Amélie Darsac comes from a family of wholesalers dealing in alcohol. One of the biggest businesses in the area. The link with the Fantins de Larsaudière was needed for business purposes. Cognac bottled by the family of Fantin de Larsaudière. It does sound a lot better than Cognac Darsac. Everyone did well out of it. The colonel found a financial cushion, the vintners a more desirable social standing.'

'A common or garden marriage of convenience. He might have expected that his wife would look for a bit of fun elsewhere!'

'It's not so simple, René. It seems they weren't uninterested in each other. They didn't have to have their arms twisted . . . But I've kept the best bit till last . . . They signed a contract when they got married. It states that the colonel inherits his wife's worldly goods. And vice versa. Amélie Darsac gets her hands on the Fantin estate if her soldier cops it first . . . It's clear that if anyone wants the other to disappear it must be the colonel . . .'

'Well done, Irène. You're unbeatable. Did it take you a long time to reach this conclusion?'

She sensed the irony and began to lecture me, as she did every time she was annoyed. 'What I mean is, she's the one with the money. If she decides to go for a divorce, Fantin is left without a penny and the cognac without a name. You get the drift. That's how she's got him under her thumb. What would you do in his place? You don't give up the millionaire life so easily, especially not the way things are going now. If you ask me, the clause in the contract relating to his wife's premature disappearance must go through his head every time he takes a little snifter.'

'To recap, you think that Fantin is planning to murder his wife and that he's using me to prepare an alibi for himself.'

She gestured with her hands to show that this was self-evident.

'And why not?'

This was the only question to which I had no answer. For most of the day I was preoccupied by the possibility that Fantin was playing a double game. Bob made his presence felt early in the evening as I was having a coffee. He was calling from Saint-Denis.

'I've got good news for you. Your client is flaunting herself at a night-club in Rochechouart, Le Bois... Congratulations, you won't get bored with her...'

'What do you mean?'

'She's larger than life. Over the top in every way. She's lengthened her name: Amélie Fantin de Larmentière or something along those lines... She spends money like water, and keeps the waiters happy, she's generous with her tips. Her fancy boys are happy too. She specializes in pilots. There's nothing better to get your mojo working.'

'Do your Australian clients write your scripts? They're not too hot... Do you think she'll come tonight?'

'Yes, she never misses. Are you going to show up there?'

'I wouldn't mind... Can you dig me out an airman's uniform in my size?'

'American? English?'

'French? I don't even know how to fly... I might as well keep the risks down.'

I waited until ten o'clock before going out. Irène was happier staying at home with her nose in a book. I walked as far as the Square d'Anvers. Despite the freezing cold and a miserable hail, all the benches were taken up by tramps, women of an indeterminate age. Legend had it that this was a meeting point for retired theatre people, singers, dancers, music hall stars, actresses, all disappeared from the boards because of wrinkles and illness. They ended up in this square with dyed hair and pancake makeup, keeping each other up on their latest plans, their unlikely come-backs.

The fleece-lined jacket kept me warm. In spite of heavy pressure from Bob I hadn't pinned on the insignia of the 8th fighter squadron. I was keeping it in reserve in my pocket. The military police still raided the area regularly. What a piss-off to find yourself behind bars for using a uniform illegally.

The Bois was in fact a private club hidden discreetly behind a façade. It took up practically the whole of a little street leading to the Avenue de Trudaine, on the smart side of Pigalle. The well-to-do apartment blocks that surrounded it certainly held an impressive number of pimps and madams. On the other side of the boulevard the girls were killing themselves in order to pay the rent.

I looked the joint over carefully. It was impossible to slip in unnoticed. A hefty bouncer was pacing up and down the pavement pushing aside the oglers. I gave up the idea of getting any closer for fear of being spotted, then slipped down to the garage on the quayside.

The boss was tinkering around with the engine of a 1907 Model T Ford. His own. He glanced at the jacket;

'Hi. Carnival's early this year... You've come for your plane?'

'You got it... You look after your old banger and don't ask any questions. Have you checked the petrol?'

'No. If you need some, I've got a can in the boot. Take it, I'll add it on to your bill.'

This was a subtle way of telling me that I hadn't wiped the slate clean for the last two months. I picked up the hint.

'Do you want me to buy you some chalk?'

I'd forgotten that he liked a quick dig.

'There's plenty of that. It's more a question of finding room on the blackboard!'

After I'd checked the roof was well fixed, I took the Packard out. Fifteen minutes later I stopped right outside the entrance to the Bois. I let the motor idle and went up to the welcome party.

'Take the car round to the garage. Has Mme de Larsaudière arrived yet?'

The guy stared at the car without moving a muscle. I turned the screw.

'I take it you know how to drive at least?'

'Of course, sir. I'll take care of it. As for the rest, I'm sorry but we don't know the clients' names. Management orders.'

I plunged through the revolving door. The maître d' approached me while the cloakroom attendant glanced disdainfully at my jacket. Nothing in it for her. You didn't leave a ticket-to-ride like that in the cloakroom.

'Have you reserved a table for one?'

'No, I came on impulse but some friends might join me later.'

The corners of his mouth turned up, sketching out a smile but he caught himself in time. 'In that case, follow me. I've still got some space on the left of the dance-floor. Do you like music?'

I pretended not to have heard him. I couldn't see myself discussing jazz or tango with the waiter. It didn't match up to the character of the gigolo I was supposed to be playing. He showed me to a corner table on the main route to the toilets. Not surprising that it was still free!

I took advantage of being next to the toilets to go and fix my medals and turn myself into a flying ace. As soon as I found my seat again I ordered a bourbon that I paid up front, at the same time as slipping a generous amount to the guy in the white jacket. When he brought the glass I asked a few questions.

'Do you think you could discreetly point out Mme de Larsaudière to me, when she comes; I'd like to get to know her.'

He gave me a conspiratorial wink.

'You're not the only one queueing up … That's her over there, at the round table. There's only one like her, you can't make any mistake.'

I stood up to get a better view. There were five people at the table, two women and three men.

'There are two women.'

'Unfortunately, she's not the young blonde. She still looks good for her age …'

Given all my medals, I had faced out far more formidable dangers. I took my courage in both hands, and stood up at the end of the dance, a fox-trot. I did a tour of the room, to win a bit of time. The range of punters surprised me. All the other night-clubs in Pigalle went for a clash of style, an alliance of opposites: whores and millionaires, high society and low life all thrown in together. Here, at the Bois, the whole spectrum was represented, with not a single level missed out. National unity played as nocturne.

Two orchestras were sharing the stage: a jazz band whose musicians pretended to jabber in English with a Belleville accent and a group with a more mellow style which specialized in covers of the current stars, Spinelly, Mistinguett, Florelle.

The counterfeit Yanks attacked Jim Europe's 'Too Much

Mustard' in Dixieland style. Their effort wasn't bad even if the trombonist announced the name of the piece as 'Tremoutarde'. Thanks to Bob, I had the original at home, as well as a 1914 cover version, which Irène had found in the flea-market at Saint-Ouen.

The ragtime rhythm emptied the tables in a flash. They all shimmied in rhythm, one breast after another. A corset salesman would have made his fortune standing at the exit of a night-club like this.

Fantin's wife didn't join in this ritual. She preferred to draw out her face-to-face, or more precisely her mouth-to-mouth, with a young guy who looked like my brother: slicked back hair, brown leather jacket, epaulettes, flannel trousers, patent boots…

Except that his medals were a real part of the outfit. Top of his class, by all appearances. The trick would be to know what my ranking was!

The young girl from their table was on her own on the edge of the dance-floor. I decided to go up and invite her to swing together. I didn't give her a chance to tell me that her partner was just paying a quick visit to the toilet and dragged her among the other couples. Waves of warmth perfumed with Cologne and sweat rose from the naked backs and shoulders as the dance twirled round. The stench of a cheap dive…

When the number finished, the pianist went on to a solo version of Nick La Rocca's 'Livery Stable Blues'. He fingered the keys almost as well as Henry Ragas but, to be quite honest, I would have preferred to enjoy it sipping my bourbon with Blondie in a quiet corner. Instead of this idyllic vision, we were jammed in the middle of a swirling mass of damp evening suits and low necked gowns working themselves loose, all topped by reddened faces.

A violent blow in the back from a woman high enough to confuse the blues and a beguine pushed me against my partner. No need to use my hands to appreciate the outlines of her anatomy. I stayed close in until the end of the song, she seemed to find the contact to her taste.

'Would you like to come and have a drink at my table?'

'It's difficult, I'm with somebody. It would be better if you came and sat with us. Anyway, you'll all have something in common, there are three other pilots.'

I had just had time to bone up on the technical details of the Spad VII, the rising star of Guynemer, Fonck and Co... I had to stay on the ground: if they took off, I was done for... I barely knew the difference between a joystick and a propeller!

The ace of all aces was still engrossed in sucking on my client's lips, the second, whose blonde I had just pinched, came back from the toilets just as the last of the group dropped into his seat, made breathless by dancing three numbers on the trot.

The flight team was complete. In retrospect it would have been better to play my cards close to my chest.

In less than an hour I had gone over every detail of the old plane, the bodywork, the wingspan, the 180 horsepower Hispano-Suiza engine, the firepower, the 7.65 calibre Vickers machine-gun in synch with the propeller.

I lobbed in the usual piece about the Spad's lack of manoeuvrability due to the lengthened wingspan which was luckily compensated for by an improved ability to climb.

'As for the dives, the less said the better... They were the pits!'

The two aviators left and my partner listened to me politely. As for the couple, after two abortive efforts I gave up hope of interesting them in my mad aerial adventures.

I began to wonder if Mme de Larsaudière had even glanced at me during the hour I'd been at her table! Just before midnight, she got up, still hooked up to her gigolo. Truly, a kissing marathon. They went over to a door hidden by a green velvet curtain, to the right of the orchestra. They had their backs to us but I had the distinct impression that the aviator put his hand to the inside pocket of his jacket, looking for his wallet. They disappeared, having settled up. I leant over the young woman's naked shoulder.

'Are they leaving already?'

'Are you from the sticks or what?'

'No, it's just that it's the first time I've set foot in this club. Are you going to explain?'

'There's nothing to explain. If you want to understand, you'll have to do the same as them. Do you fancy it?'

I indicated that I did. The most likely story was that the owner had put an illegal gambling den in his back-room . . . I must have had 500 or 600 francs on me. Not enough to enjoy some heavy gambling but I could keep the pretence up for a little while. The blonde stood up.

'OK then, let's go.'

It cost 50 francs each to go through the curtain. I paid up. The girl seemed to think this the most natural thing in the world, as if it was in the nature of things that she should never have to get any money out. She'd better not count on me for a handful or two of tokens . . . We were greeted on the other side of the door by a hostess who gave us a room, number 25. I was only just through the door when the blonde, whose name I still didn't know, stripped naked. She didn't even bother to play poker! I began to have a serious reaction as her breasts appeared and I followed suit, throwing my disguise in a heap on the floor. As soon as I was suitably undressed I held her close, without any preliminaries, trying to regain control of my breathing. She pushed me gently away.

'Don't be in such a hurry, we've got plenty of time.'

She opened a door at the back of the room which led into a vast and dimly lit room. I stepped into the unknown, my prick leading the way. I found that I was at one end of an oval-shaped room whose walls were punctuated by fifty or so doors which each led into a room like ours. The space in the middle was taken up by several low platforms with mattresses and bright cushions where a few couples were writhing around. I was suddenly overwhelmed by a bitter sick feeling as I recognized Mme de Larsaudière's flaccid back going up and down to a rhythm set by the pilot trapped beneath her.

My thoughts took me back to the trenches three years ago where other bodies writhed feebly... the same ghastly nakedness... the same cries and moans.

All desire had drained away. I went back to the room under my partner's curious stare. She was on the brink of asking me why but changed her mind when she saw my expression. There was nothing romantic to be found there! I quickly got dressed again, without saying a word. When I got back into the dance hall, the old-fashioned orchestra was having a go at one of Carco and Yvain's signature tunes.

'To have someone under your skin
Is the worst of all ills.
But that's to know love
As it really feels.'

I took a detour past my table to empty the glass of bourbon. The maître d'hotel sat a couple down as soon as I left. The joint seemed to be hopping.

Not a soul in sight outside. Even the bouncer had disappeared. Just my luck: how could I find out where he'd parked my car?

I didn't have too much time to dwell on the question. A much more urgent problem was pressed on my consciousness.

The two most recent friends of my client—and of the blonde girl too—suddenly detached themselves from a doorway and blocked my way, seeming pretty annoyed. The smaller of the two, about as friendly as a grenade without a pin, looked me up and down.

'So, you're an ace from the 8th fighter squadron?'

An ace, perhaps that was a bit steep... As for the rest, it was better to keep the story spinning.

'Yeah, so what's your problem... Have you got German ancestors somewhere? That would explain your bad temper.'

'That's a good one! What we don't like one bit are shirkers who strut around disguised as airmen and steal girls from under our noses. We've been through enough to have earned the right to take first pick. Understood?'

I should have been waiting for it. It was a classic move: his foot shot out the moment he finished his little tirade. No escape! The tip of his ankle boot made contact with that part of my person that had carried itself so proudly only a few minutes previously. Winded, I doubled over, and felt the pain spread through my whole abdomen. I forced myself to breathe through my nose in short bursts. I managed to blurt out a few words.

'I can explain everything ... It's not what it seems.'

The second kick got me just as my knees buckled to the ground. A marksman's precision: just under the ribs, on the solar plexus. I toppled, asking myself just what stupid comment I had let slip to make them so sure of themselves.

It was Bob who fouled up. That would teach me to find out more for myself and to trust my friends less. Yet I knew enough guys who could have told me that the 8th squadron had been disbanded by General Nivelle in May '17, after it had been decimated by German snipers at the Somme.

The aforementioned general would have been surprised to know that the only survivor had had his face smashed up in the Rue Rochechouart, after a failed orgy!

I was out for the count. A shower of melted snow woke me up a few moments later. The doorman had reappeared. Like magic. He helped me up.

'Did you slip, sir?'

He had the clear, steady gaze of a chief screw who had just been promised the governorship of a prison.

'No, I got jumped by some guys who were probably after my wallet.' He pointed to the outside pocket of the jacket.

'Amateurs ... they missed their chance.'

I pulled a note out of my leather wallet.

'OK, let's not talk about it any more. Go get my car. I'm going home, it's not my lucky day.'

I followed the overhead metro to La Chapelle. I didn't have

the spirit to trail into the garage with my Double-Six. I left it outside in the snow, hoping that the asset-strippers would have fingers too numb with cold to be working that night.

I made a big mistake: I was missing a wheel by the next day. I pondered deeply as to what the hired thief would do with a radiator cap and one rim! At that rate, he would be in a right state before he'd got himself together a whole Packard.

I invited Irène to lunch chez Julien, a bistro in the Saint-Denis area, before taking her to the cinema, the Gaumont-Palace. In the middle of the film, I suddenly realized that in a confused way, I was trying to make up for my night at the Bois.

She hadn't asked any questions, even when I let out a shriek of pain when she stroked me a bit too intimately. Yet I wasn't in the habit of doing such a thing…

The documentary that preceded Charlie Chaplin's *The Pawnshop* was ironically titled *The Way of Agony*.

What a programme!

CHAPTER 3

I had met Irène six months before. At most. She'd answered one of my ads in the paper about my photographic file of amnesiacs. Three lines in heavy type in the classified page of the *Excelsior*, just below the wedding announcements.

At that time I didn't receive my clients in the flat on the Rue Maroc. The internal decor would have made them turn tail. I found it handier to fix up appointments in the bars of well known hotels or cafés.

I was particularly fond of a joint called La Cigale on the Boulevard Poissonière. They greeted me like an old friend there. I even had the use of a table at the front, which impressed the women who came up from the sticks and fell into my net.

Irène didn't let herself be taken in. I quickly realized that here was something different; right from the start she let it be understood that she wasn't married.

'I'm not looking for a husband.'

In a way I was relieved at this, she was much too pretty to throw herself into retrieving a basket-case... She threw the newspaper on the table, folded open to show the page where I had put my ad.

'So you're the one who puts out these messages?'

I passed my eyes over the announcement.

The Griffon Agency. All manner of enquiries.
SPEEDY DIVORCE.
Specialist in men who disappeared on the frontline.
Photographic file.

There followed, in small letters, my telephone number. I ordered a John Collins, while her fancy settled on a cocktail it would never have occurred to me to drink, a Kiss Me Quick.

I had a feeling that this wasn't just because of the taste of this concoction. What followed proved me right.

'Yes, I'm responsible for this ad. I'm René Griffon. If you're not married perhaps you're looking for an absent lover or relative?'

'No, my father and one of my brothers came back... in pieces, but we had time to identify them before... That's why I wanted to see your face. I couldn't imagine what a bastard who profits by other people's unhappiness could look like.'

There was no point in arguing with this hysterical woman. I got up and took down my jacket from the wall. I took a detour via the bar.

'Put my drinks on the bill. If this young woman wants something else, it's on me.'

I left and went up the Boulevard towards Porte Saint-Denis. I had no wish to sit through a sermon... no matter who it came from! What did she know about my life and other people's unhappiness? Nothing. All she'd done was weep for her father and her brother, then deck herself out in black... a colour that suited her very well.

I had every right to say such things, I'd paid the highest price.

With interest.

I wasn't stealing their money—quite the opposite, every one of them owed me, for the rest of eternity.

The mint at the Bank of France could have churned out 1000-franc notes for a whole year, without even beginning to make up for just one of those nights in hell. Not one! Try as I might not to think about it, I found myself back in that cursed trench near Thierville, ten of us squashed together without a hope of regaining contact with our lines. Shells, both ours and the ones in front of us, were blowing up incessantly. Clods of earth sodden with water or blood exploded into the air every time a bomb landed on one of the thousands of bodies rotting on the plain. We'd even given up wiping ourselves down. I kept myself on my feet, my hands clenched so tightly round the butt of my gun that the fingers were bloodless.

Night had followed day, without dusk, going from grey to black. At about eight o'clock the sky was streaked with rifle fire forerunning the deluge of fire and lead.

A young Breton was the first to crack. I didn't know his name, only that he came from the country round Quimperlé. The report from his Lebel was covered by the whistling of a heavy shell. He fell at my feet, his head all bloody. The bullet had gone in under his chin and out through his helmet in a dead straight line. At this very moment his name must be chiselled in granite on some monument facing the town hall of his God-forsaken village... Two soldiers in bronze with their cloaks lightly dusted with green throw themselves cheerfully forward to assault the enemy lines... that is unless they preferred the image of the weeping widow bent over the disjointed body of a dead child.

They were so sure they could keep the heroic image...

Howling with despair, I picked up the smoking gun. No one moved a muscle as I smashed in the miserable Breton's skull with the butt of his rifle. They thought I was mad, you can tell the pitying looks people give to those whose behaviour strays beyond the boundaries. I had to do it. For his sake. Didn't they understand that?

Some bureaucrat would have wormed his way out of the department in charge of calculating the losses, who would have been only to glad to have discovered a 'suicide', a coward who had chosen to die by his own hand rather than face up to the German bullets!

Lousy bastard, it was your skull I was thinking of as I reduced that young boy's to a pulp.

I had to do it. Even if it didn't mean very much to have his name engraved in stone. Even if it was only for a mother's peace of mind, a memory of him kept alive by a woman. A number on a pension list, blunting the fear of being reduced to paupery.

I didn't have much time for sermons even before August 1914...

I had no business near the Porte Saint-Denis. I did an about turn. Irène caught me up in the Passage Jouffroy, before the exit from the Musée Grevin, just as I was about to step into the doorway of a sauna that served as a front for a brothel. No one but a blind simpleton could have mistaken the dual role of this particular bathing establishment; there were several young women permanently on display in the entrance hall. One glance, and you could see that they had no need to freshen themselves up.

I pretended to be admiring the architectural assets of the place.

'I am sorry I hurt your feelings...'

'Let's say you came close. What were you running after?'

'After you. I wanted to thank you for the Kiss Me Quick.'

'The what...'

This only conveys the half of my astonishment: she spoke English with a heavy accent. Quice meu Kique...

'That's what the "coquetaille" you bought me was called. I don't know what it means.'

It wasn't hard to turn myself into an English language teacher. I'm unbeatable in any practical demonstration. Her kiss tasted of the finest malt whisky. She broke out of my grip and pushed open the door of the sauna.

'Did you want to go in here?'

I found it difficult to imagine myself choosing the goods with a stranger in tow, even if I was already in love with her.

'No, not really. Did you?'

She burst out laughing and put her arm through mine. An hour later, she was organizing our life together. Down to the last detail.

In exchange for somewhere to live, she insisted on taking over the office management. With one exception: cooking, shopping and housework would be taken in turns. With some swops allowed.

She informed me that she didn't want to have any children, explaining that she took her own precautions in this matter... A doctor who was part of a neo-Malthusian birth control group put a kind of membrane over her uterus every month. One day she wanted to show it to me, but she gave up when she saw my reaction. She let out a petulant comment at this scene in our sexual life together:

'If women made the same fuss every time they were faced by the most ordinary condom!' It was a new kind of delirium; up to now I'd been used to checking on the calendar while the woman took her temperature before we could take any action. A veritable clinical ritual interrupted at the crucial moment by 'Get out quickly! I'm not sure.' With no regrets I traded in this anxiety for the magic membrane, as soon as it would stay in position. Irène's decisiveness made sure that I had little chance of becoming a father in the near future.

It's difficult to make plans for nine months ahead when your biggest ambition is to get through the day in front of you without even thinking about whether there'll be a next. Our relationship had been going for six months without any major hitches, just a few rows when Irène tried to palm me off with tins of corned mutton when it was her turn to cook. The telephone was ringing when we came home from the cinema. I immediately recognized Fantin's cut and dried tone of voice.

'I want to see you as soon as possible, M. Griffon. I've been calling your office for the last hour. Can you come straight away?'

'I've just got in, let me catch my breath. Can't it wait till tomorrow?'

'I pay you well enough to be able to make demands on you. Come at once. It's of the utmost urgency.'

He said these last words with feeling. I couldn't imagine that the colonel would put on such a performance just to get a detective to keep him company.

'Can't you tell me a bit more about it?'

He breathed deeply. I felt a sob about to break through.

'My daughter has just tried to poison herself.'

'I'm on my way.'

I hung up then put on my warmest clothes; it could be a rough journey. The sky was getting more and more leaden, with the promise of snow hanging heavily in the air. I kissed Irène.

'Give the garage a bell, so they can get the car ready. Bye, see you later.'

'Try to come back in better shape than last night, you're a private detective, not a eunuch.'

The roads had emptied at nightfall and the wind was rattling the panes in the streetlights. My path was crossed by a few rag-pickers out with their carts loaded with greyish shapes. They had plenty of work after a holiday... The area was unusually quiet, the silence broken only by the howling of a few dogs at the car's approach.

I nearly drove straight into a column of foot-soldiers who were going back to the fort at Aubervilliers: the beam on my headlights was adjusted a bit low. I made a note to tell them tomorrow. As soon as we got past the Courneuve I abruptly felt myself on the edge of the French plain, met by the bitter damp cold that sweeps across the flat countryside all the way from Belgium, from Picardy, and ends up running up against the outer walls of Paris.

An old running-mate, this cold I fought against with all my soul...

I reached Aulnay at about nine o'clock. The gate had been left open. I parked my car behind the house. I was getting familiar with the place already!

When I went into the house Colonel Fantin was having a discussion with a severe-looking person. A doctor presumably, if his leather briefcase bulging with bottles and instruments lying on the armchair was anything to go by.

Fantin avoided introducing us to each other. He waved me into the kitchen until he'd brought his discussion to an end.

A salami was lying abandoned on the table. I cut myself a few thin slices while taking in the décor. The warm cossetted atmosphere of the dining-room was paralleled by a spartan comfort. Presumably this was good enough for the servants!

I opened a blue door hoping to find some well-stocked shelves. No such luck… once again I found myself staring into a stand-up toilet crudely built into a not very useful corner of the kitchen. It was only ten metres away from the one that I'd confused with the exit last time I was here! Each to his own: the class struggle goes on even in the squatting position. The colonel burst in just as I was about to avenge myself on the unfortunate salami.

'I was feeling a bit hollow… You called me just as I was about to sit down to eat.'

'You'll find some bread in the sideboard.'

I asked him a few questions as I made myself a snack.

'Was that the doctor? What does he have to say about your daughter?'

He nodded his head, obviously tired.

'Yes, our family doctor. According to his observations, she had ingested a large quantity of laudanum. Thanks be to God, the amount was not sufficient to endanger her life… She will most probably be very ill for two or three days.'

'Laudanum! How did she manage to get hold of such stuff?'

He crossed his arms nervously behind his back, then began to pace round and round the kitchen, stopping to answer my questions.

'It's my fault. I keep some permanently in my room. A phial.'

'Is it for your own use or your wife's?'

'Mine, of course. I was wounded. Like many others. When the pain becomes too much, it's the only medicine that can touch it. Luce must have known … I've never hidden it, it would have never occurred to me that she could have …'

'Now you know! I want to see your daughter. Where has she been taken?'

'Nowhere. She's sleeping in her room. There was no need to transfer her, according to the doctor. It wasn't crucial to pump her stomach out. Go ahead, but first I would like you to be frank with me …'

I would like to have slipped in that as far as frankness was concerned, he had a bit of a cheek … You don't take laudanum just to ease the pain of old wounds. I knew more than one person who hung on to his bottle as tightly as an opium pipe …

'I'll try …'

'Could this accident have any relationship to the task that I entrusted to you?'

I couldn't see where Luce fitted into the picture but it was true that the coincidence between the start of my investigation and her suicide attempt was a puzzle.

'It could be. Especially as your wife's friends weren't wearing kid gloves last night. I'll tell you later. Take me up to her room. Is Mme de Larsaudière around?'

He could hardly avoid answering although he looked as if he wished he could.

'No. She went out just before all this took place. I don't know where to contact her.'

'I'll give it a try. Can I use the phone? In private …'

The colonel didn't rouse much sympathy in me, but I still

couldn't imagine ringing up Le Bois under his nose just to interrupt his wife's manic man-eating, while his kid was raving under the influence of laudanum on the next floor above.

Mme de Larsaudière didn't seem to be surprised to be rung up by a stranger who moreover seemed to be very familiar with the way she spent her time.

The lack of surprise should have put me on my guard, but I wasn't expecting a dirty trick. It's always tempting to be too naive when it comes to dealing with people who've been through the same bad experiences as yourself.

I was whispering, convinced that Fantin was listening in, his ear glued to the keyhole.

'You must come home immediately. It's about your daughter.'

'What's happened? Has Luce had an accident?'

They were certainly trying to hang on to this version of the story.

'No, it's not too serious ... She tried to kill herself but she's out of danger. She needs you with her.'

I hung up without giving her the chance to draw the conversation out any further. Fantin looked at me enquiringly.

'She's on her way. She'll be here within the hour. Leave me alone with Luce. I'll call you if you're needed.'

Her room was on the first floor, at the end of a gloomy corridor that smelled of saltpetre. It was a moderate sized room hung with pink flock paper. There was a stucco moulding all round the edge of the ceiling. There was the same motif, a garland of flowers, around the central light suspended from the ceiling. The bed was weighed down by a pile of pink muslin. A real sugar-bowl.

An impressive collection of little girl's toys was piled up on the shelves and furniture: cuddly toys, little cradles, dinner sets, dolls, as if this twenty-five-year-old girl had kept every toy from her childhood going back to her first rattle! She only needed to put in a phial of laudanum to complete the picture.

You wouldn't expect anything different if you were bringing up a half-wit. I took in the décor, then my attention was caught by a heap of clothes flowing off the back of an armchair. Everything had been flung down as it came off and a padded bra topped the heap. The hired nurse who sat white and still near the bed could see by my expression what had caught my attention. She reached out an arm and covered the bit of underwear with the fold of a dress.

There was nothing prudish in the gesture. There was more pity: she had understood how much of the unexpected and painful this intimate garment revealed. Luce was still pretending to be a little doll, but now the little doll had her periods! There is nothing more desperate than someone clinging on to their childhood. The picture I had seen the other day on the piano said it all. Luce's face was already marked by the lost battle against time.

I leant over the bed. She was sleeping, her features drawn against the tangled hair. Even with her eyes closed she still maintained that air of tragedy which the photographer had caught so well.

'Do you think she'll wake up soon?'

I spoke quietly, influenced by the death-bed atmosphere emanating from the nurse's uniform.

'No, not until tomorrow. Laudanum is excellent for sleeping.'

'There's no way to speed up her return to consciousness?'

'No, none. Anyway sleep is the best thing for her. She was looking for oblivion, she found it—temporarily.'

I left, slightly bothered by the unpleasant pharmaceutical smells. Colonel Fantin appeared at the head of the stairs as soon as he heard the floorboards squeak.

'Well? Did she speak to you?'

'She's sleeping like a log. I'll speak to her tomorrow.'

'Yes, that would be better. I would never have forgiven myself if Luce had died. Never.' Without a moment's pause, he pulled himself up and changed the subject.

'As a matter of fact, what were you talking about just now, when you referred to some violence of which you had been the victim?'

'It comes with the job. We stick our noses into everything, we're bound to get them flattened every now and then. I followed your wife. She spends a lot of time hanging around a few particular joints in Montmartre, surrounded by flyers. It's quite the fashion at the moment. It's a world full of sharp dealers who know how to smell out a good con. In short, there's a lot of possibilities to choose from…'

'And the fight?… Did they find out who you were?'

'No, they thought I was poaching their game. They were defending their territory.'

Fantin turned to the window and parted the curtains. The window-pane misted up in time to his breathing.

'You haven't got any leads yet. Be honest.'

That was a good one! I could see dozens of leads, but when it came to following the right one, that was a different kettle of fish.

'I've no intention of turning myself into a punch-ball. I

like to fight back. There's just one golden rule: don't rush in. I could leap in feet first and come back with any old solution. I'd rather make sure that that wouldn't end up in a stream of reprisals. For example, I'd be really pissed off if what your daughter has done had anything to do with what happened to me last night… She's only a child.'

He left his lookout post to lead me into the kitchen.

'Come and have a drink, we'll talk about that later.'

'I'm right behind you. I wouldn't mind a bite to eat as well. That snack seems a long time ago.'

'I'll see to it. The cook is looking after Luce.'

The colonel settled himself in front of the stove. Without asking me, he made me a cheese omelette. By a stroke of luck, I like them. I cleaned the plate in three mouthfuls.

'I'll come back tomorrow morning to try and talk to your daughter. I don't know if I'll get much out of it. She might still not be up to much.'

'In that case, stay here tonight. You don't want to go all that way for nothing in these icy conditions. The telephone is at your service to notify your absence.'

I accepted his proposal. There was just one drawback to it; the risk of a confrontation with the noted Mme de Larsaudière. Even though she'd spent the whole of yesterday evening tangled in a clinch with her airman, she must have taken me in, even if only in the most hazy way. I wasn't dressed up as a ridiculous flying ace any more, that might be enough to put her off the track. As for me, I couldn't get out of my head a picture of her clinch in the oval room at the Bois.

I didn't have long to wait before I was put on the spot: the silence was broken by the purring sound of a Renault taxi.

The door was thrown open to allow Mme de Larsaudière to make her entrance. This woman looked quite different from the one who, only an hour earlier, had been vamping young men. Her makeup was awry, her eyes were reddened by tears and her arms and head moved jerkily, a picture of someone deeply distraught.

She didn't notice me and spoke aggressively to her husband, in a harsh, strident tone. 'Where is she? What have you done to her?... My poor little girl...'

The colonel tried to take a grip of her shoulders and calm her down, but she shook him off, avoiding his touch. He let fall his hands and looked at me in despair.

'She's up in her room; she's sleeping. Dr Langlois has just left. There is no need to worry...'

She rushed up the stairs to be by her daughter's side. The colonel led me to the guest room without saying another word, leaving me alone with my questions.

CHAPTER 4

I immediately fell into a dreamless sleep. The windows of the room overlooked the garden and the sun was already warming the window-panes when I woke in the morning. A thin covering of snow had fallen in the night. I stood at the window to survey the scene and get used to the light. Someone other than myself would have pondered over some philosophical considerations which are said to help in life.

I was just about to splash some water on my face when the colonel and his wife appeared by the cars, my Packard and their Vauxhall. I hadn't heard them coming up, as the sound of their footsteps was muffled by the carpet of snow. They were talking heatedly in low voices. I eased open the latch and half-opened the window, but couldn't hear more than a few words here and there: they were talking about me. Mme de Larsaudière said 'Detective', the colonel said 'Griffon'. The state of their daughter's health was also a focus of their conversation.

I was reassured to find that the colonel was quite frank with his wife about me. Irène's hypothesis didn't hold water any more. In order to use me as a smokescreen Fantin would at least have to keep my mission secret. To be honest, this had bothered me and I was glad to be quit of this plot out of a cheap melodrama.

Fantin fussed around the English car and got it going, but

it was Mme de Larsaudière who got behind the wheel on her own. She eased the car into first and rolled slowly round the corner of the house.

I got into my clothes quickly. Once out in the corridor I decided to knock on Luce Fantin's door. No answer. I turned the handle. The young girl was still sleeping. She stirred, disturbed by the squeaking door. The armchair where the sick-nurse had sat was empty. I made myself comfortable to wait for Luce to wake up. I coughed from time to time so that I wouldn't have to wait too long... She decided to lift her lids at the tenth round of pretend coughing. She tried to lift her head over the pink muslin counterpane without being able to hold it in place. She fell back on the pillow, as if the whole effort had been too much for her.

I came closer to help her sit up in bed.

'Who are you? I want to see Dr Langlois.'

She spoke in a monotone. A tone that could give you the blues for a whole week. The same absence of feeling as those wounded who were begging you to finish them off. Towards the end.

'The doctor's gone. He'll be back this afternoon. He told me to look after you, I'm his assistant.'

'When did he go ...?'

'You've been sleeping for thirteen hours straight. It only needed a bit more ...'

The technique wasn't exactly above board, but the woolly state of the young girl gave me a unique opportunity to get information out of her that she would never tell anyone once in full possession of her faculties. I had to work quickly before either the father or the cook burst into their 'little invalid's' room.

'You shouldn't be trying to kill yourself at your age... It's the first time, isn't it?'

I asked her a whole series of questions, each more bland than the last without being able to get Luce to spill the beans. I circled round her defences without being able to find one weak spot. A fortress! I had even taken on that nonchalant manner that medics have when they want to conceal from you that they have just found a cancerous tumour in its terminal phase... 'And how's work going, is it still OK?'

I stumbled on to the road in by pure chance, totally surprised to find it where I least expected.

'You know, everyone's worried about you. They love you. Your mother came rushing home as soon as...'

She cut my sentence short. She sat up in bed, her eyes lit up with sudden fury.

'Don't talk to me about her. I hate her! I don't want anything more to do with a mother like that...'

The trickiest part was over. I won her over with elaborate stories of my own youth, without hesitation I invented hypothetical relationship problems with my family, spicing the whole lot with theoretical insights into the difficulties of puberty and how much more difficult it was to communicate once adolescence was reached.

I blurted out enough idiotic statements to get her to confess. Luckily, there were no mirrors in the room; I wouldn't like to have seen myself.

In this sodding line of work, you had to develop some immunity from your own stories while you were investigating, or risk fucking up. The same farce in a cell at La Roquette, no problem, you make up a reason.

It was impossible to keep your distance in this cocoon of pink muslin and toys, impossible to stay calm while listening to a half-doped kid crying out her disgust with life and calling for her mother's death.

'She's never been interested in me. She gets rid of me by giving me presents. I only have to ask for something and she thinks she has to buy it for me. Last time I said I would like to learn how to ride ... He arrived the next week. The most beautiful thoroughbred. All I wanted was just to go for a little canter. Nothing more!'

'That's no reason to kill yourself. It shows that she thinks a lot about you. Doesn't it?'

'No, it doesn't. I don't exist, anyway, nothing exists for her outside of this business of Cognac and pigs ...'

'What pig business?'

If Luce knew all about her mother's night-time excursions, that changed everything. That was enough to make much tougher children lose their balance. But I was barking up the wrong tree.

'This business to commercialize American pork. They talk about nothing else at meal-times.'

'Surely it's not these pigs that have brought you to such a pitch?'

She shrugged her shoulders.

'No. It was those horrible photos ... My mother with Emmanuel ... She gave me one of her leather bags as a present last month ... I must have said I liked it or something like that ... It was hanging in the cupboard in the corridor ... the one between my room and hers. She must have made a mistake, forgotten that it belonged to me now. I found her compact and some papers inside. They hadn't been there that morning. I was going to put them on her dressing-table, but I had a look, out of curiosity. There were photos of her with Emmanuel... I could have died on the spot. You just can't understand...'

The confession had drained her.

'Where are they?'

She shook her head.

'I don't know.'

I had noticed a bag hung on a hook behind the door. I grabbed it and felt around inside. Nothing.

Luce turned away, her face buried in the pillow, her body shaking with sobs. I was about to leave the room when the 'nurse' burst in. She gave me a reproving look and knelt down by the bed.

Fantin was seated in an armchair in the drawing-room. I interrupted his perusal of the financial news. I told him about his daughter without managing to make him let go of his paper. Once he'd got over yesterday's shock, the movements of the Stock Exchange again took first place in his preoccupations. I persisted.

'I think quite simply your daughter is having a lot of difficulty in forgetting somebody...'

The colonel lowered the paper to his knees. The smell of ink floated in the room, wafted here and there by the draughts.

'Where do you get this idea? I've never seen her with a single boy. Luce has always been very reserved, you could even say shy. The life of the daughter of a career soldier is not as easy as people think... I haven't been present as much as I should have been.'

'None the less it seems to me that she's well hooked on a certain Emmanuel. Do you know who he is?'

He abandoned his paper for real and put his thick glasses down on the table.

'Yes, I know him. Emmanuel! It's unbelievable. The poor little thing!'

He spoke in tones of doom which matched the expression on his face.

'What's the matter? Is he dead?'

Fantin got up, indicating that I should follow him.

'It would be better... He was my batman during the war. I took him everywhere with me, on my postings, on leave. He has lived in this house for weeks at a time, on several occasions. I never noticed anything between Luce and him...'

'Perhaps nothing ever happened. Love is sometimes as silent as the greatest sorrow... Does this Emmanuel come back to see you from time to time?'

'Unfortunately for him, it would be quite impossible: he was very badly wounded at Montdidier, in August 1918. A German counter-attack with incendiary bombs. His whole group was decimated. It would have been better if he hadn't escaped... He's tied to a bed for the rest of his days, his arms torn off, his trunk and face atrociously burnt. A living corpse... He was being looked after near Amiens, in a special hospital. As soon as he could be moved I found him a place near here, at the sanatorium in Villepinte.'

'A sanatorium is for tubercular people, not major burns.'

'Nowadays they mostly look after people who have been gassed... They deal with those in most need... It's an establishment with a high reputation, run by the Association of the

Sisters of the Assumption. They have shown an admirable devotion to all these young boys. Luce goes to see them every week... Let us say that I always attributed her interest in their suffering to Christian charity. There was nothing to show...'

'Unless you think that love is a higher form of charity.'

To tell the truth, I didn't give a damn. The best organized Christian charity begins at home. That was my entire philosophy. We had come back to our original starting-point, the little drawing-room leading on to the hall.

I had been wanting to have a piss ever since I'd left the bedroom. Politeness can push back the limits of endurance, but that's all: it cannot abolish them. I broached the subject of the toilets. Fantin pointed at a grey door half-hidden behind one of the pillars of the bookshelf. Yet more toilets... The Fantin family must surely be the supreme consumers of hygienic equipment!

To think that every room had one...

I relieved myself before taking my leave, my hands still damp. Despite the cold, the Packard started up with the first turn of the motor. I stopped as soon as I saw a café with a phone. The owner of the Halte du Chemin de Fer entrusted me with his phone directory for Aulnay, where I found Dr Langlois's number. He was still in his surgery, just about to set off on home visits. I passed myself off as a close friend of the family and pretended to be asking for news of the colonel's daughter. To gain his confidence, I reminded him of our brief encounter the day before, when he was expanding on his diagnosis with Fantin. 'It'll all be forgotten in a week's time. That young girl needs a breath of fresh air. I advised her father to send her up into the mountains. There's nothing better for a touch of nerves.'

'I'm happy to hear that she's out of danger. No one can be protected from such a stupid accident! It will be a lesson to the colonel not to leave his flasks of laudanum that you prescribe for him lying around...'

The worthy man didn't give me time to finish my sentence. He reacted sharply.

'Who told you such stories? I have never prescribed anything of the kind for Colonel Fantin. Laudanum indeed! In fact, in his state it would certainly not be advisable...'

In great confusion, I apologized before hanging up. A good piece of work. The café owner couldn't get over finding a customer in such great good humour at the onset of a day which seemed set to break all records for cold.

Straight away I set off towards Villepinte. Everyone had heard of Villepinte at least once in their lives: it was one of the biggest concentrations of tuberculosis sufferers in France. There were five hundred sick people there permanently, which doubled the local population. Otherwise there was nothing but fields. The thousand hectares of the commune were shared out between three big landowners. The most astute of them (who, by pure chance, was also the most important) had managed to get himself into the good books of the hospital management. Through this he had the post of mayor, re-elected every time by the bundles of votes that were placed in the ballot box by the sisters and the medical staff. There were only a few conscious votes among the hundreds of proxies signed by the confused invalids who would never know which candidate received their vote.

Once past the last houses of Aulnay, there was nothing but

open land. A plain in every sense of the word. I was tempted to turn off the ignition and just coast along, but the headwind was too strong. There was not a single mound of earth, you could gaze out in each direction from the paved road over extensive cultivated fields. There were still here and there in the furrows patches of frozen snow. According to the map you had to turn left, after a combined café and petrol station. I slowed down to take the corner as soon as I passed the sign of the 'Rouergats' then crossed the seedy allotments cultivated out of the water-logged land by the workers from the lime quarries of Vaujours or Livry.

The imposing red brick mass of the sanatorium dominated the skyline: you didn't expect to find such a huge building in a God-forsaken spot like Villepinte. The sisters hadn't stinted themselves: it was a real country mansion in the Louis XV style in the shape of a horseshoe that enclosed a formally laid-out garden. An old church was propped up in one corner of the building. The bell-tower of a chapel matched it on the other side. The town hall was not far away, in the middle of a little square of beaten earth planted with leafless trees. Well, it was a surprise but you got used to it pretty quickly! In fact, the most remarkable sight was the number of small bars that completed the picture: Le Relais de la Poste, Au Clairon, Chez Mortalet, Au Rendez-vous des Flamands, and yet others that you could guess were hidden in the back-streets. There were twenty of them at the very least! I chose Les Flamands.

I was propped up against the bar for at least five minutes before the bartender decided to glance my way. His service was as reluctant as his accent was incomprehensible. I ordered a glass of beer so as not to upset his routine too much. The clientele must have been mostly agricultural workers who had come down from Belgium. The absence of spittoons indicated that the hospital residents chose to frequent the other establishments around the square.

I tried to start up a conversation while sipping my beer.

'What time do visiting hours begin?'

'One o'clock.'

He yawned as he answered.

'Until when?'

'They shut up shop at six in the winter.'

There was no point in going on, it was obvious that rhetoric wasn't his forte. I swallowed my beer in one gulp and killed the rest of the morning before visiting-time hanging around the village. You could do great things to your lungs in this part of the world: I could feel my wind-pipe freezing every time I took a breath!

To help me pass the time, a shepherd decided to lead a herd of at least a hundred sheep down to the river Sausset along the beaten track that led to Tremblay-lès-Gonesse. Rising above the bleating, the church bells rang out to visitors that the doors of the hospital were now open.

There wasn't much of a crowd, two couples and a woman dressed in black came out of the cafés as I tracked back to the hospital. I was the last through the gate. At the end of the curve of buildings the park was bounded by a wall of a formidable height. In the middle of the lawn there was a platform with a metal framework, partially filled in with glass, which enabled the invalids to get some fresh air and warm themselves in the sun's rays. With a bit of imagination they could pretend they were at the races!

At the beginning of the afternoon, the place was quiet and deserted.

A nun dressed in grey, her head constricted by a wimple, came to meet me.

'What can I do for you, my son?'

Really it was an obsession, they always saw you as if you were still in short trousers!

'I've come to see Emmanuel Alizan…'

My sentence hung in mid-air. It was beyond me to end it with the traditional 'sister'. I knew that she was waiting for my response and that it only needed this simple word to become part of the game. I didn't give a shit that she thought I was being rude when actually I was just hesitating between 'Madame' or 'Mademoiselle' without being sure which of the two titles was the most appropriate.

'The staircase on the right, first floor. You will find him in the wing reserved for those with major wounds.'

She couldn't help sweeping me from head to toe with one of those looks dripping with pity monopolized by the career faithful. I turned on my heel to get away from her but I could feel the full power of my hostess's commiseration on my back. The corridors were cluttered with trolleys overflowing with dirty plates, medicine, linen. I went down them at a fast trot so that the terrible smell of bruised and bandaged bodies wouldn't cling to me. Both to right and left, the doors were open on to the repulsive sight of empty sockets and amputations.

I made myself look straight in front of me. Over the last two years I had tried to forget the day to day unfolding of the war. I wanted to believe that I had come out of it unscathed. I knew enough people who only lived through a nostalgia for that butchery, always ready to set off for a new round just like in '14…Their house full of trophies, German bayonets, pointed helmets, copper shells, etc, down to the Hunnish tibia dug out of a trench after a victorious assault. Just for fun, one of these idiots had shown me the last traces of meat…just before getting my fist in his face.

Emmanuel Alizan was one of the few inmates to have a room all to himself. His name was framed in a transparent panel within the half-open door.

I was about to push it open when I noticed that a nurse wearing the uniform of St Mary the Helper was bustling around the wounded man. I leant over slightly, my face level with the edge of the small net hung between the frame and the door. She was in the middle of bathing the man I had come to see. The hideously mutilated body of Emmanuel Alizan was centre stage, laid out on an iron bed, completely naked. Fine brown lines ran the length of his chest, thickening around what was left of his upper limbs. The man's face was now nothing more than chaotic scar tissue, swollen by the emergence of the jaw and two intact rows of teeth.

The nurse was walking around the bed, a large sea sponge in her hand; she wiped his skin with quick, deft movements, taking care not to drag the raw flesh. She had just finished rinsing his chest and turned to dip her sponge in a bowl filled with a bluish foamy liquid.

At that precise instant something unbelievable happened. Almost certainly used to the immutable order of the toilette, the wounded man's body was getting ready for the second stage of the cleansing: the pelvis and legs…

Emmanuel began to move feebly and to moan while,

imperceptibly, his sex swelled and rose until it was suddenly upright.

At that moment the sister turned around to face her patient, her hand extended, ready to carry out her duties.

My eyes glued to the crack, my breath held, I couldn't stop looking at Emmanuel's member. The nurse was suddenly very angry: she pressed the sponge on top of his erect penis and abruptly pulled the sheet down over this young mutilated person.

'You're disgusting. Do you think it's nice to look after boors like you ... If that's the only thanks you're going to give us ... You're incapable of any kind of self-control even with someone in a habit like me ... I'm going to report this and from tomorrow on it'll be a male nurse looking after you. Then we'll see if you calm down a bit!' Little by little the desire disappeared under the sheet. She had been right to choose to take holy vows but she was worthless as a nurse.

I could easily imagine the intense humiliation that Emmanuel Alizan would feel, but I couldn't see what I could do or say that would make it any better. I got up and gave three short knocks on the door. A brief command was my reply.

'Yes, come in.'

I had some trouble looking the sister in the eyes without crying out my disgust at what I had just seen ... I would have done better to study my toecaps: before me I had one of the most beautiful girls I had ever had a chance to meet, a face to make you visit all the convents in France.

'What do you want?'

'I'd like to have a talk with M. Alizan, if that's possible.'

'You can try ... He hasn't said one syllable ever since he was wounded. But it's always possible for a miracle to happen. You think they're completely finished and then they come back to life... One wonders why...'

She went out and I was left alone with this silent mummy. I went up to the window and, with my forehead pressed against the cold pane, I began to cry without understanding clearly why or for whom.

CHAPTER 5

'What's the matter, son, is there something wrong?'

I turned round. An inmate of the hospital stood in the doorway. He didn't look at all like an invalid and his massive shoulders stretched the striped cotton of his pyjama top.

'It's nothing, just a touch of the blues ... Seeing him in that state ...'

'Yes, it's not a pretty sight. If it was up to me, I'd leave him to die in peace.'

I looked at the wounded man, expecting some reaction.

'What if he heard you?'

'No chance, his ear-drums were pierced, torn to shreds. Are you a relative?'

'No. I'm following up an inquiry in which he plays a small part. I happened to be passing by.'

He stepped back.

'I'll leave you in that case. I don't like to disturb ...'

'You don't like the cops either! I'm not one of them. Private detective. I'm working on my own account.'

'You're doing the job under direct contract, bypassing the state ... Not a bad idea. The squaddies should have thought of that in '14, I wouldn't be here scraping out my lungs to get rid of all those blasted traces of mustard gas. People talk about the good healthy air you find on the Marne … I've never been able to get used to the country! And you, M. Detective, were you involved?'

'Involved in what?'

'You haven't heard about the match between France and Germany … You sound like you've come out of mothballs!'

'No, I was on the pitch. Down in the mud when you think about it! Three years at the front, that's a long lease … But strangely enough, I've got just one idea, to forget all about it.'

He came nearer. His breath stank of cheap canteen wine.

'You're not like your friend's mate …'

He pointed at the wounded man with his chin.

'Every time he turns up here, we all have to go on parade … Brave foot-sloggers and all the rest. Even the ones who are flat on their backs are allowed out for an airing.'

'Who are you talking about?'

'The colonel! They don't make two like that … Fada de la Grenouillère or something along those lines … Double-barrelled handles aren't my strong point. To be frank, I prefer his wife. Furs, silk stockings, nothing better to lift the troops' morale, if you know what I mean … With her perfume in the corridors, it's a breath of life even if it's only up your nose … She's not one of the youngest any more, but I fancy her more than her daughter … She's like the gate to a prison! Anyway, the big man doesn't give a shit. All he cares about is the march-past!'

'Do they often come here to see him?'

'Yes and no. The two women each come once a month. The colonel waits for the holiday at the beginning of October: the hero comes to see his troops march past! Some army; nothing but a pile of broken bones. They wheel out the cabbages on their beds, the ones that can't even move their little finger ... Anyway, it makes a change from the usual grind and it's an excuse to get a free drink at Mortalet.'

'Do you know the colonel well?'

He sat himself down carefully on the very edge of the bed, just above the frame so as not to disturb the wounded man.

'You could say so! I had him on my back for two years ... I was even there when his batman got that Russian shell smack in the face!'

'What Russians? He got caught in a German counter-attack in front of Montdidier! By a grenade ...'

'You too, they've been feeding that story! August '18, the final offensive ... The man wounded in the last quarter of an hour ... Fuck that! This thing didn't happen in the Somme but in the Creuse, in September '17! That makes quite a difference, doesn't it?'

The poor guy must have made up some story so that he could slip off quietly to the Mortalet. He was over the top ... It was the first time anyone had ever told me about a French-Russian war in autumn 1917 in the Creuse! Why not a world championship boxing match between Foch and the King of the Pygmies!

'I'm sorry to tell you that, but I think you've got your wires crossed. The Russians were on our side against the Germans. They stopped laying out on the war when they had their revolution, at the end of '17, not before. I know what I'm talking about, we had one of their regiments supporting us at Verdun ...'

He raised his head with a smile.

'You can't lecture me ... I know all about these massacres, young man ....'

There couldn't be more than a few months' difference between us. A year at the most, but at that moment I found it quite natural that he should take on the role of older man. He paused a little before continuing.

'I was part of the expedition, up to La Courtine. There were two thousand troops: infantry, gunners, cavalry, plus two artillery sections. Size 75 cannons.'

'Where is La Courtine?'

'I've told you, in the Creuse! In the south of the region, just before the Haute-Vienne. You can call it the plateau of Millevaches, if you prefer. Forty kilometres from Aubusson. I should know, the train dropped us in the God-forsaken area and we had to cross it on the hoof! There were twenty thousand Russians in the camp. One to ten. To be fair, we had some Russians on our side as well...'

I looked at Emmanuel Alizan. He seemed to be asleep. His toughened eyelids covered practically the whole of his eyes. I sat down in the chair reserved for visitors.

'Your story isn't very clear... There were Russians everywhere... Lenin could have declared independence in the Massif Central!'

'I'll start from the beginning, it'll be simpler. In '16, the State began to run low on cannon-fodder. You can replace shells, but men are another kettle of fish! They filled out the lines with Africans, Senegalese, Algerians, but it wasn't enough for them to decimate two continents, they had to drag Asia into it... The Tsar was a better bargain as far as human flesh goes. He footed the boat ticket for forty thousand of his old serfs, dumping point: Marseille. We had a carnival for them on the Canebière... First a celebration, then they get the coffins out!

That was at the beginning of the summer, then, to work… Off to the Champagne… Except you had no right to the liquid version… You had to make do with gas! That sobered them up quickly. The first time, when Kerensky had his revolution, they showed the white flag… A Russky strike smack in the middle of the front! What a mess! It turned out it was full of agitators: workers from the outskirts of Moscow. The Tsar must have taken the opportunity to get rid of all these shit-stirrers. In any case, the State decided to transfer them to the rear, to the camp at La Courtine, to make sure the infection wouldn't spread…'

'And what's Colonel Fantin got to do with this whole story?'

'Hang on! Paris wasn't built in a day… You have to take your time… If I want to be understood, then I have to be precise. That's my philosophy. Right: once they were shut up in La Courtine, the Russians began to elect soviets and to turn on their officers. It was a powder-keg. Especially as they'd all kept their arms… Their general, Palitzine, a Whiter than White Russian, came close to being lynched. When that happened the loyalists left the camp and the French Government decided to wipe out the rebellion. That's where I come into the picture: Colonel Fantin had been given orders to march on La Courtine with some of the regiment. We took up our position on the hills at the end of August. A line of cannon. Ultimatum. All those who agreed to give themselves up would be treated with clemency. The others would face court-martial… Fewer than two hundred gave themselves up. The next day we evacuated the civilian population within a ten-kilometre radius, then the artillery began to shell the camp…'

'And what did they do, when faced with all this? Did they reply in kind?'

'No, nothing at the beginning... They sang Chopin's "Funeral March", the "Marseillaise", the "Internationale"... Then they began to dig trenches to protect themselves...'

'The bombardment went on for a long time?'

'Pretty much. Four days and four nights... On the last day the Russkies decided to fire on us. No more than ten shells at the most. Fantin's batman...'

He waved his hand at the wounded man.

'... he copped it carrying a message to the front lines without any cover... We really didn't expect them to be taking potshots at people...'

'How did it finish... with an attack?'

'No, they were only trying to save face. They gave themselves up soon afterwards... You have to admit they were screwed... They had nothing to drink, nothing to eat. With thousands like that, hollow belly and throat dry, you can't go on for years! Afterwards, we buried the dead all together... A good dose of quicklime instead of a funeral oration...'

'That's drastic! What did they do with the prisoners?'

'The mutineers? They were sent to Africa to the hardline battalions. Except for the leaders; they were handed over to the Russian authorities stationed in France. You can guess what happened: twelve bullets each. Curtains. To come back to my story, you don't win medals with this kind of campaign! We were forbidden to talk about it until the end of the war... That would have got us into real hot water... Even the graves of our boys in the cemetery at La Courtine were unnamed, just marked with a wooden cross...'

'You must at least have been given a long leave after such a job?'

He lifted his head and looked at me pityingly.

'Are you dreaming or something? Once that diversion was over, they pushed us on to the front line, into the most dangerous sections ... As if they wanted to wipe us out. Everyone who'd been party to this Red affair ... They didn't miss their target by much ... The 296th may be the most decorated regiment in the world, but what they don't tell you is that it also has the highest record of losses. Hardly any slipped through ... I knew one other beside myself, Julien Versois, a great guy, a lad from Gers. A livewire. He snuffed it here just like that. Last November, round about the 11th! He probably couldn't stand their charade in the Champs-Elysées ...'

I was just about to fire another question at him when the sister reappeared.

'What on earth are you doing in this room, M. Leduc? I was looking for you everywhere for your treatment ... If this goes on we'll have to turn you out. We don't keep convalescents for ever. There are plenty who would be only too glad to take your place!'

He got up and stalked off down the corridor, shrugging his shoulders.

'I know, I know, Sister ... I was talking with the gentleman ... It's very rare, in this day and age, to find people who are prepared to listen.'

His reply was accompanied by a heavy wink in my direction. I followed on his heels and slipped a 5-franc note in the palm of his hand as I overtook him. Not for his information, he hadn't asked me for anything. I just thought that, if I were in his shoes, it would give me pleasure to feel a bit of connivance.

I kept my eyes glued to the ground as I went down to the

steps, determined to get away from this gloomy hospital as soon as possible, but the head sister caught me in the doorway.

'Could you leave me your name? We have a list of visitors and invite them to take part in our annual celebration. It's in October... Our sick ones always look forward to this time with impatience...'

I stopped dead, rebuttoned my coat, put on my gloves, taking plenty of time to form a reply. The sister waited, the compassionate smile graven on to her waxen mask.

'I hope I may take your name in exchange. I'm having a little party on the first of May... I'm sure it would give you some ideas on brightening up the atmosphere...'

The wax turned to marble. Markedly less indulgent. Apparently, it was not the first time she'd had an encounter with the devil.

On the way back to Paris, I took a detour by way of the American warehouse at the Pleyel crossroads. Bob was glued to the phone, apparently busy negotiating his percentage on the next shady deal. He rolled his eyes to tell me how important the conversation was and that he mustn't be interrupted. I nobbled him as soon as he put down the receiver.

'Not bad your scheme to disguise me as a pilot.'

'Hey, not so fast... It was your idea... I just supplied the uniform... You didn't run into trouble, did you?'

'No, no problem... Unless, that is, you think that a bit of healthy punishment comes under the title of "a problem"... A first-class beating! You could have found out where the insignia came from ... The squadron had been disbanded for months ... It didn't take them long to smell a rat.'

Instead of excusing himself, he burst into laughter.

'So that's it! I wondered what the catch was with those insignia! It was some deal, they slipped me a box for peanuts ... I picked up your idea and flogged the lot off to would-be Romeos ... There's going to be a few broken noses around!'

I forgot about my anger. To hear him talking in slang with a Chicago accent was enough to put me back in a good mood.

'Have you got anything handy to make it up to me?'

Bob began to ferret through heaps of material, of papers, odd bits and pieces that were lying around the room, haphazardly uncovering empty boxes and cartons.

'Yeah .... You should like this. I've just had some "jeans" come in. The real stuff, quality clothing. They've come straight over from San Francisco, California. How about it?'

Whistling a cowboy tune, he grabbed hold of a tailor's tape and measured my waist and my height up to my bellybutton. Then he plunged into a rapid mental calculation.

'You must be a size 33/36, unless I've ballsed it up. Try these on.'

He threw me some dark blue trousers made of material as rough as a canvas tent, whose pockets and waistband were studded with copper rivets. Sinuous shapes were visibly outlined on the bum and fly in white stitching, giving a suggestive effect. I tried on the 'jeans'. Bob knelt down to adjust the turn-ups.

'Fantastic. You'll see, they're very practical. You can't wear them out. You're a real cowboy! I've got some smaller sizes ... Take a pair back for Irène, I'm sure they'll suit her as well.'

He thought she was Calamity Jane! Without much enthusiasm, I wrapped my presents up in a back number of *Figaro*. I would have much preferred a little something from a raid on some bourbon or Virginia tobacco! But as they say, a bird in the hand is worth two in the bush!

I went home, feeling a bit tired and frozen to the bone, my blue-jeans under my arm. There was a surprise waiting for me in the sitting-room. Irène was not alone. A tall blond boy was sitting on the sofa next to her; I could just make out his profile against the wallpaper behind, but he was half-hidden behind the leaves of a huge indoor plant. Greens in a flower-pot, a hobby of Irène's. I could sprout fifteen spots on my face and she wouldn't notice, but it only needed one of her plants to go slightly yellow, on the back of the leaf, and she would bring out a whole gamut of treatments.

Irène quickly gathered that I would have preferred to meet her friend another time.

'René, can I introduce M. Dahvof... M. Dahvof is conducting a survey in our area. He's trying to set up a group of Esperantists... Don't you think that's interesting?'

I suddenly decided to show my grumpy side.

'Yeah, I believe you. Is that what he's ranting on about?'

The guy came out from behind his leafy disguise, unfolded himself and said goodbye. He promised Irène he would come back and see her. She closed the door behind the visitor and turned round to face me.

'Who do you think you are? Why are you behaving like this tonight? I've never seen this man before. They've been knocking on all the doors... they're anarchists...'

'That's a good one... I've had a foul day at a hospital...

Nothing better than a nice threesome to restore my spirits! What exactly are they doing, these Esperantists? Picking up women at home?'

'You sound like an idiot! No, they've invented a universal language. So that all nations can talk to each other … It's very idealistic, isn't it? Anyway I think it would be a great step forward.'

I was stung by her last few words.

'A step forward! No question, it's great to move on! Less than twenty years ago, tens of thousands of people rallied together to applaud some stupid idiot who had just crossed the Channel in a little plane … Drawing people together, aviation in the service of peace … They played a trick on us … In two seconds, some clever dick realized that it would be ever so cunning to use it, as they went overhead, to drop a couple of bombs if the opportunity arose … Another one racked his brains to perfect a machine-gun linked to the engine so that they could fire through the blades of a moving propeller! You can't stop the great move forward … It goes in leaps and bounds …'

Irène didn't seem over-impressed by my tirade.

'You're an expert, it's great stuff; carry on with the subject!'

'Yes, but it's not to my credit: I was a pilot for an evening, in the middle of the week …'

'Is that what made you so sensitive?'

I knew exactly what she was referring to. I reassured her.

'You sly little thing … It's getting better. It's just as well because I've also just invented a universal language …'

Soon after we were going over the first lesson. When school was out, Irène filled me in on what was happening at the agency.

Dead calm. The 100 francs daily from Colonel Fantin were

most welcome. I summed up my day to Irène, then told her that her idea of Fantin plotting to kill his wife had bitten the dust.

'They were talking about me to each other this morning, without realizing that I could hear them. They're playing cat and mouse: Fantin won't introduce me to his wife, who knows exactly who I am! And now their kid is trying to kill herself because the mother has seduced her lover... Not to mention the father, who's trying to take me for a ride about a bottle of laudanum that he's never had... It can't be the massacre of the Russians at La Courtine that's set off all this havoc!'

Irène cut me short.

'It's not as stupid as all that! If you think about it carefully, the only link between all these stories... is your invalid, Emmanuel Alizan. He was the colonel's batman, wounded on a secret mission, the wife's lover and the object of the girl's undeclared love... There's only one problem...'

'What's that?'

'Given your description of his state of decay, it's out of the question that he's the one who spends his time writing anonymous letters and using them to extort money! Unless he's passing on orders to an accomplice! This is beginning to be like something out of Fantomas!'

Up to that point I had drawn back from the idea of telling her about the horrible scene I had witnessed at the hospital, through the half-open door. Out of selfishness. So as not to spoil those moments of pleasure we had just shared. On impulse I plunged in, my eyes lowered to the sheet. Irène heard me out in silence. When I'd finished, she got up and dressed, with no explanation. She stopped at the front door.

'Take me to see Louise, Place Clichy. Is the car downstairs?'

I nodded to show it was before sliding into Bob's jeans.

The Louise in question reigned over the entrance to a squalid passageway, a couple of steps from Wepler. Rue Capron, the last stop for Parisians before being relegated to the suburbs or the badlands around the old fortifications. It wasn't hard to spot the toothless fifty-year-old, her breasts marbled with prominent veins. The most surprising thing was that she was never out of work and rarely stayed more than a quarter of an hour at her post on the corner of the Avenue Clichy.

We had to wait for the end of a session. Louise was overjoyed to see us and dragged us into a smoky bar crammed full of regulars who all greeted her.

Irène urged me to tell Emmanuel's story once again. It was beginning to be a drag, especially as an old boozer on the table to my right couldn't stop staring at me and eyeing Irène and Louise. He must have had us down as a trio of perverts. Finally I came to the end of my story. Louise looked me up and down.

'Is this your idea?'

I looked at her enquiringly, but Irène gave me no time to reply.

'No, it's nothing to do with him . . . It's down to me.'

'Anyway, it's OK by me. I know what I have to do.'

Irène got up to thank her.

'We'll sort out the money . . . The fare there and back as well as . . . Well, we understand each other . . .'

I was completely lost until Louise vehemently refused Irène's offer.

'Out of the question! The one time you ask a favour as a friend, I'm not going to put the meter on! These sanctimonious nuns, they're real bitches!'

She left with this parting shot.

Ever since then, she takes the train once a month to visit Emmanuel Alizan. There must have been a few questions asked about the moral behaviour of certain acquaintances of the grossly mutilated patient.

But those rendezvous did him so much good…

CHAPTER 6

I returned to Aulnay the very next morning with the firm intention of confronting the colonel with a few contradictions and bent on finding out exactly what he thought he was up to.

After the meeting with Louise the night before, I had left the car once again in the Rue Maroc, out of laziness.

Unluckily for him, my accredited expert in stolen pieces must have knocked off work that night: the Double-Six seemed in one piece. Driving through the suburbs was quite uneventful, apart from the customary bottlenecks at the cattle market due to the arrival of beef destined for quartering.

I had left early, just before eight o'clock and the shutters of the Rue Thomas were still closed when I arrived at Aulnay. I was about to go into the first café open when the postman came out of an alley, a hundred metres further down.

A postwoman, in fact, in her dismal blue uniform and straw hat with a grey ribbon on which I could make out the inscription POSTE in capital letters.

She went up to the gate and stood on the tips of her toes in order to reach the Fantins' letterbox and push in a bundle of magazines and letters.

'No need to go to such trouble; I've come to see the colonel. I'll deliver his mail into his own hands in time for breakfast.'

I was rewarded with an official smile followed by the pile of stamped letters. Mechanically, I looked through them one by one.

The Fantin family subscribed to every publication touching on military organization, methods of viniculture or of breeding porkers! At least it reminded me that dear Mme de Larsaudière didn't just dabble in three star brandy but that she was also involved in the buying and selling of pig meat. A large chunk of the letters came from organizations of veteran soldiers, officers' associations. Invariably, the left side of these missives was decorated with various emblems of war. Sabres, grenades, bombs, helmets, all the paraphernalia... Plumb in the middle of this lot I came across a white envelope which simply had the name and address of the colonel. I could identify immediately the type of machine: an Underwood similar to the one which had been used for the anonymous letter which Fantin had shown me.

The date stamp revealed that it had been posted the evening before, at six o'clock in Aulnay.

I hid myself in the space between the two pillars of the door in order to get out of the postwoman's field of vision. I wanted to know the score!

I stuffed the magazines and the rest of the usual mail back in the box and hurried to the station. I was pretty sure of finding a café open. I ordered a toddy before asking for the toilets.

It didn't stink too much; I took as long as was needed to open the letter according to the rules of the game. Inside was a page of text that could equally only have been typed on an Underwood:

'I know that you've hired a cop. There's no point as I've decided to call a halt. Meet me tonight at twenty-one hours at the exit from Roissy-en-France. Don't forget to bring 100,000 francs. To close the account.'

I bought a pot of white paste in a stationer's to close the envelope without trace and returned to the Fantins' house. I slipped the letter in among the others before I rang the bell. I wasn't waiting long. The colonel himself came to the gate. I pointed my finger to show him that the postman had been by. Grumbling he unlocked the door of the box.

'What a pile of useless paper! I barely read half of it…'

Once inside the house he sat himself down in front of his breakfast and began the task of going through the mail. I tried to stay calm as he was sharing it out but my eyes were fixed on the corner of white paper visible under the pile of magazines.

Finally the colonel picked it up and put the blade of the letter-opener underneath the flap so recently stuck down. I watched his face. Fantin limited himself to clenching his jaw and tightening his eyes. If I hadn't known what was inside the letter, I would almost surely have noticed nothing unusual.

I thought I could make out the ghost of a smile, then he put down his letter and set to work with gusto on another bit of bread.

He chewed his bread dipped in coffee without paying me the slightest attention. I broke the silence in the clumsiest way possible. It seemed like I couldn't open my mouth without saying something stupid!

'Still no news of your blackmailer?'

'What made you think of him?'

I realized the brick I'd dropped. I had to make good my mistake quickly.

'Nothing in particular. In this sort of case, quite often when a private eye starts poking his nose in it triggers off a response. They're very suspicious of the least thing, these blackmailers. As soon as there's a whiff of something in the air they tell you to ease up or they'll blow the gaff...'

'Are you as visible as all that, M. Griffon? I see no evidence that you've flushed out the quarry! In fact, I find you very discreet...'

'It has to be said that you're not helping me as much as you could, colonel. For example, you could have told me of the relationship that your wife had with your old batman, Emmanuel Alizan. That would have saved me a day's wasted journey to Villepinte, that waiting-room of death.'

He picked up a second piece of buttered bread which he spread with jam. The morsel hovered two inches from his mouth.

'Yes indeed, I should have done. Believe me, I didn't want to hide it from you, but I couldn't bring myself to tell you... It's not as easy as you seem to think to confide the story of the failure of one's private life to a stranger... Even if the stranger makes a living out of confidences of this kind! I didn't have the courage, M. Griffon, and, to be frank, I don't think I would have liked to have had...'

It was hard to know if he was being honest or not! On the surface, there was no doubt he was playing the role of the mortified cuckold with conviction. The most experienced actor of the Comédie-Française would have been taken in! Except that pinned under his elbow he had a letter of prime importance to me of which he never breathed a word... This was becoming bloody awkward! I felt I owed it to myself to cut through the shit.

'Yes, I suppose in the end you imagine that it goes without saying. There's nothing worse than getting stuck in a rut. On the other hand, there was nothing preventing you from telling me about your mission in the Creuse, against the mutinous Russians. Not only did you pass over this episode in silence, but you went so far as to palm me off with some fantastic story: that Emmanuel Alizan was wounded in August 1918 when in fact he took a shell full in the face at the camp at La Courtine. I don't know why you're behaving so mysteriously, the war's over ...'

'Not against the Reds! Our soldiers are still fighting them, it behoves us not to forget! Was it Leduc who put you in the picture? I'm sure it was him ... He just likes the sound of his own voice. I will remind him that he's still in the army.'

'What are you frightened of? You were following orders, weren't you?'

'I am not frightened of anything! It's just that this mission was classified as a military secret and that classification has never been lifted. At that time, in September 1917, it would have had the worst possible effect on the troops who held the front line to announce that the Russian regiments had mutinied and were taking orders from Bolshevik agitators. We never recognized Lenin's terrorist government and the legal authority over the Russian expeditionary force lay entirely with General Palitzine. In any case, the mutineers, or at least those who refused to swear allegiance, are still in Africa in the most authoritarian battalions ... They will stay there until legitimate power has been re-established on Russian territory.'

'That doesn't seem to be around the corner; they announced the fall of Irkutsk in the papers this morning ... the White armies are fleeing Siberia ... It feels like the end ... Apart from all that, did the Russians at La Courtine know that they were facing French troops, and not other Russian loyalists?'

'Yes. I negotiated with their head, Baltaisse and their political commissar, as they called him, Globa... I wasn't much in favour of this exchange but Painlevé, the Minister of War, insisted. A waste of time: in the end we had to use the only method that would prove effective against these barbarians: cannon-fire. There, you know everything about this episode. It wasn't the most glorious moment of my career... I felt sullied at being pitched against cowards and mutineers while our men were writing in blood the finest pages in the history of France. A soldier must fight or die. No alternative! In any case, what connection can there be with the blackmailer?'

'One can't overlook any possibility. Suppose that some Red soldiers had remembered your name, that they'd followed your trail ever since the end of the war... It wouldn't be surprising. I can easily imagine a group of conspirators jumping on the episode at La Courtine to set up a bit of extortion...'

The colonel got up, and wiped his mouth to get rid of a few breadcrumbs on his lips. He made sure he picked up his mail before heading for the staircase.

That's an absurd hypothesis. Secrecy was absolutely essential during the war for reasons of morale. It has stayed a secret simply for reasons of politics... Leduc could tell you about it without running into any danger... I recognize my weak spots in relation to my private life but I have never wavered in matters of military honour. As the status of secrecy was maintained, I would never have been the first to broach the subject. Put this story to one side and pursue your pilots... I have the feeling that that's the right trail.'

With these words he mounted the stairs two at a time, giving me no chance to ask about Luce.

I had the feeling I was wasting my time in this house. The day was half spent but I wasn't tempted to take a stroll around this residential suburb. A quick look round the copper plates and stone façades was enough to lower my spirits.

I treated myself to a burst of speed on an open bit of road between Le Blanc-Mesnil and Le Bourget. The needle touched seventy. Without any strain. Nothing like it to calm your nerves.

Unless some moron with his cart chooses that moment to cross your path at a slow walking pace... There was no way to avoid a collision. The horse must have sensed the approaching danger because he reared up as the Packard came closer. I stamped on the brake at the same time as I turned the wheel to the left to go round the trailer but I was coming up to it too fast. The tyres skidded on the wet ground and, with a screech of scraping metal, the car came to a dead stop against the wooden side on which was inscribed the wagoner's line of business:

Maison Landros.
Supplier of ice for cold storage.
Since 1873.

Furious, I got out of the Double-Six.

'What the fuck are you doing delivering ice in midwinter?'

'What about you? Where do you think you are? On a racetrack trying to set a record... I'm a working man, Mister!'

I inspected the right side of my car. The mudguard in front had suffered as well as the chrome strip on the running board. More of a fright than actual harm. As for the wagon, that had lost a few grammes of dust... I put on my haughtiest manner.

'OK. We'll leave it at that. It's just a question of bad luck!'

As I took the first bend to the right, I realized that the tyre was binding on the bodywork. I straightened it out with the crank and limped along at thirty an hour to the garage down by the quay. The boss was incensed when he met me.

'What have you been doing to ruin your little runner... You have to hold on to the wheel when you've got an engine like that under the bonnet!'

'Thanks for the advice. Now tell me what I should do when a cart cuts in front of me, right under my nose! Go into reverse?'

He was already tapping the metalwork, leaning under the chassis. His voice floated up to me, distorted by the echo from the inspection pit.

'The paint's scratched... Nothing really serious. You're not the first... There are crashes all day long in Paris. They're going to make regulations. They want to enforce everything at the same time. Two shy guys at a crossroads, they'd be waving each other on for ever. Two hot-shots and boom! There's a smash... One or the other, no one gets by and you get a free concert of car-horns thrown in. Have a look at Caumartin, they've made a one-way street.'

'What's that, a one-way street!'

'I'm speaking French, aren't I? You're not very on the ball for a private detective... One-way: you're only allowed to drive in one direction.'

'And if you want to go back the way you've come?'

'Well, you take another street. You go round the area and you come back further up, in Rue Caumartin.'

'People will never agree to it! Even trains go in both directions... I'll go take a look one day, it must be worth the gas. To come back to other things, I need the car this evening. I'll come by around seven. Will you be done?'

He stroked the bonnet of the Packard with affection.

'Come by at seven. I'm not going to leave her in this mess, poor thing! You'll have to leave her with me for a couple of days, as soon as possible, to touch up the paintwork.'

Irène was on her own, the Esperanto-speaker having cancelled! Laughing she threw herself into my arms.

'You're free... We can have a little holiday: he's paid for you to have next week off. Will you take me to the movies?'

I got my breath back.

'OK, so I'm free. Nothing new... What's going on?'

'Your colonel of Who knows where...'

I corrected her: I don't like my clients to be taken so casually.

'Fantin de Larsaudière.'

'Yeah, sure. He telephoned to thank you and to tell you to stop your enquiries. Everything's sorted out. He'll be sending you the money today. Two full weeks at 100 francs a day... Are you pleased?'

It took me a little while to understand what Irène was saying. Fantin had decided to finish the game on his own! No client had yet dared to insult me by taking me off a case. Within a hair's breadth of success. It's as if someone stole your bride as you were coming out of the town hall...

'Does he think I'm some kind of amateur! I was taken on to solve a case and I'll take it to the end... I don't need his charity: he's paying me to the end of the week, OK, but I'll work to earn the dosh whether he wants me to or not!'

'If I understand you rightly I shouldn't put the file away.'

'Out of the question! Fantin has a date tonight with his blackmailer; I intercepted the letter... I'll tell you more later... Half the time, these society meetings end up in a gun battle! I'll take a discreet look around there. If everything goes smoothly, we'll have another think about the file tomorrow.'

I pushed open the door of the bedroom and stretched out on the counterpane, heels propped on the copper bedrail, my head resting on my hands.

It grated on me to become a busybody. Irène's voice made me jump just as I was dozing off.

'Tell me, you did say that, as well as cognac, Fantin's wife was involved in societies dealing especially in marketing pig meat...?'

I enunciated a husky:

'Yes.'

She came up to the foot of the bed and threw *Le Temps* at me. It unfolded as it landed on my chest.

'Read page five, it should interest you. Some bloke has written an article on the subject. Of course she hasn't been quoted, but it's worth finding out more.'

I ferreted out the article in question, an anonymous half-column, squeezed between news of a derailment on the Ivory Coast and a catastrophic flood in Japan. On reading it, it seemed to be nothing more nor less than a rewrite of a statement from the Ministry. A tried and trusted method of dropping a bit of ballast when a scandal seems on the point of breaking. You skilfully leak two or three indiscretions by means of the establishment papers. That's usually enough to put people off the scent. The man in the street gets the impression that, finally, the sharks are being hunted, when in fact they're already hunting in other seas.

I skimmed through the article.

STILL MORE SUPPLIES FROM THE WAR!
The liquidation of stocks from the war and past dealings with our Allies are still in the news. The most recent incident is the order for two million tons of salt pork from the United States of America, on the initiative of the Ministry of Supply.

These enormous quantities of meat were crudely designed to intervene in the markets and thus to ease speculation. It seems that there had been an overestimation of the city's ability to store meat: up to a thousand carts in convoys were needed to empty the American cargo ships in Le Havre and bring the goods to Paris.

These two million tons of pig meat represent nearly three months' work in the abattoirs of La Villette and refrigerated hangars have had to be hastily constructed. In some cases, the hangars have had to be constructed over the merchandise which, as a result, has started rotting.

Last week a convoy of twenty barges was utilized to transfer this unmanageable quantity of pig meat to an ice-making factory, which had been reopened in the middle of winter for this very purpose. A provisional, but it is hoped, definite conclusion: an agreement has just been reached with the Clairmont company which will undertake the re-utilization of this meat as canned food (pre-cooked dishes, pâtés, cooked meats) which will last longer.

My eyes came to the end of the article and travelled on down the page. The weekly snippet of municipal information declared that in the last week of December 1919, 808 deaths were recorded against an average of 845 over the year, of which 8 were suicides, 25 violent deaths, 3 criminal. There were 1064 marriages and 983 births. About 700 of these new-born were legitimate, which still left nearly 300 categorized as bastards. Free unions were wreaking havoc!

Irène shouted at me from the dining-room.

'So, you've read it... What do you think?'

'Indeed very interesting. I can well imagine her in this kind of affair. Can you imagine: two million tons! The go-betweens must be lining their pockets like there's no tomorrow. They haven't revealed for how much the meat was sold to Clairmont at the end of the line... Not very much. But their rotten tins will cost the same as all the others. Your ordinary civilian will have paid for them twice: through his taxes to finance the Ministry of Supply, and then out of his purse for Clairmont and friends! Do me a favour: go and see what's tucked in the files at the Chamber of Commerce on the Darsac Cognac Company. Maybe they've got business links with Clairmont Tinned Foods. Bottles and tins, they're often on the same shelf...'

CHAPTER 7

I was beginning to know the road from Paris to Aulnay as well as my own face! I was getting ready for the bends well before they arrived.

To be precise, I had made a little detour down the Rue Crimée to buy a pair of 'real leather' boots which Irène had caught sight of as she was strolling round the area. (There's nothing better in winter with the snow.) For once I accepted her advice without arguing, especially as they were made to go with my American jeans and my aviator's jacket.

Well set up for the worst frost!

Near the Quatre-Chemins I was held up by a strikers' demonstration. There were more and more all around the country, people were fed up with restraint. Five years of war and having to tighten your belt for the homeland... Victory hadn't changed anything on that front; the homeland wanted us to tighten yet another notch.

This time it was the margarine workers of La Villette, supported by the suet preparers and all the other workers in terrible jobs using boiling vats. The mayor of Aubervilliers, a socialist elected in December 1919, went along with his talk of solidarity, squashed between two red flags and a forest of badly painted banners proclaiming the demands of the strikers.

Misery and hard work had left their mark on the hands gripping the banner poles.

I don't know why, but there came into my mind the memory of a sordid crime committed six months ago in the sewers of Paris. Few people had paid any attention. Yet, for me, stories like this revealed far more than those eternal studies commissioned by the 'social' ministers on the moral and material conditions of life amongst the deprived classes!

The back page of the popular press could usefully replace a gaggle of distinguished researchers.

A sort of underground aristocracy had been created when the abattoirs were built. A few families of the dispossessed shared out among themselves the best 'fishing spots' where the waste pipes emptied near the Porte de la Villette. The recovery of animal matter from the abattoirs was such that, in effect, minute particles of grease could filter through, dissolved in the boiling water of the vats. Once it had gone through the drains, the grease congealed on the surface. All that was then needed was an ordinary skimmer for a miraculous harvest of tallow.

One morning in July, some guy decided, in defiance of all the unwritten rules of the professional skimmers of drains, to take up a position at the bottom of the ladder near the Rue Rouvet.

They never found out who pushed the paving-stone that had been taken up for road-works... A sewer-man found the body, half-eaten by rats, floating in the water at the main outlet, at Jaurès. No one notified the police; in that district, no one cared who the unknown murderer was... The solitary skimmer had got what he deserved. The cops obviously agreed: they were satisfied with putting the pavement back and filing the case.

The demonstrators were blocking the crossroads and letting

the cars through one at a time. When it was my turn to go through the barricade, a massive bloke with a cap pulled over his eyes planted himself in front of my tyres and began to hammer on the bonnet of the Packard and to chant:

'The filthy rich are with us! The filthy rich are with us!'

The frame vibrated as the blows rained down in time to the slogan. I stood up on the seat. No damage, for the time being; but it would be better if he wound up his little game as soon as possible. The wing, the running board, now the bonnet... Three days of this kind of treatment and I might as well be driving an old jalopy!

People were closing in, pressing up against the windows, kids ready for a bit of fun... The stewards sensed there might be a flare-up. Five or six young men, with red armbands over their coat-sleeves, grouped together to cordon off the Double-Six from the demonstrators. They signalled me to move on as quickly as possible. Apart from that, it was dead quiet.

By eight o'clock I had arrived at Roissy-en-France, a tiny village lost in fields of beetroot, between Goussainville and Tremblay. Three farmhouses, a café and about twenty windowless shacks, you could imagine yourself in Beauce... I could easily imagine the farm labourers and their families sitting round the table, eating their soup with nothing but the light of the fire. Electricity, that was just for the cinema...

I parked the Packard behind the shelter of the Compagnie des Transports Automobiles, listening out for the slightest sound. The night fell rapidly and still nothing had happened to disturb the peace in this backwood. I just had to wait. An hour after I had taken up my hiding-post, car headlights punched through the darkness.

A little Citroën, one of the new type As, stopped a hundred metres further up, on the outskirts of the village. The driver killed his lights and stayed at the wheel, his engine idling.

Silence fell once again. The man was nervous; he lit cigarette after cigarette but I couldn't make out his features by the flickering light of the match. At five to nine a new light swept over the front of the sleeping houses. Slowly the Fantins' huge Vauxhall came up the main street. Rounding a small bend, the beam of light swept over the horizon, catching for a second the chrome and windows of the Packard. I bent down, but already the lights had moved on to the Citroën, parked on the side, well in view.

The large English car parked just behind. I was just about to come out of the shelter and go further up the road, nearer to the meeting-spot, when I noticed that another car was following the Fantins', all lights out, the engine cut, moving under its own weight and the slight incline of the road.

I identified a tiny Carden... Not hard to do: this little car with a two-stroke engine and prize-winning economy had been unveiled at the October salon in Paris. Everyone spoke highly of it... but to see it behind the Vauxhall you'd think it was a lifeboat being towed by a liner!

The Carden stopped in front of the gateway of a farm, ten metres higher up and its driver ran towards the other two cars, bent over double, keeping close to the walls. He seemed young and moved easily despite his heavy overcoat. His collar, turned up to his ears, hid his features.

Roissy-en-France had never seen such traffic since the taxis to the Marne... That is if they went that way!

I waited till he was a bit further off before following his

example. I was careful to keep a respectable distance between us.

He stopped when he was practically level with the rear of the Vauxhall. He knelt down and pulled a gun out of his pocket. This was getting serious. I copied him. Just the feel of my hand on the butt of my gun, a Webley, reassured me. It's not always enough just to want to understand ... Especially when your opponents walk around armed.

I hid myself as best as I could behind the trunk of an ancient plane tree while trying to find the best spot: one from which I could keep all the protagonists in this strange meeting within my field of fire.

The front left-hand door of the English car, the one which, unlike in French cars, is the passenger door, opened. The colonel got out, a small suitcase under his arm. So he hadn't come alone. The driver's side opened next and Mme de Larsaudière appeared. A family affair ... The Citroën door slammed. A small man, dressed in grey, round glasses covering his eyes, came to meet the couple. An envelope that looked like a child's schoolbook showed up as a pale silhouette on the dark mass. They exchanged a few words and were about to go through with the handover when Fantin pointed a gun in his opponent's direction. He thought he had won the game but the late arrival jumped out of his hiding-place, like a devil, and put himself between the colonel and the blackmailer.

From then on, it all took place in a flash. Fantin launched himself at the stranger and managed to knock him over while his wife threw herself at the little man in glasses. Two shots tore through the silence. Mme de Larsaudière crumpled silently in front of the wheels of the Citroën.

The stranger had got to his feet and he took advantage of the confusion after the hail of fire to knock the colonel out with the butt of his gun before turning to the blackmailer.

The latter had taken advantage of the few seconds' respite to slip behind the wheel of his car. He crunched his gears, the wheels spun against the woman's inert body. At the second try they managed to get over the obstacle. The Citroën brushed against the plane tree from which I had not stirred through the whole drama, not knowing in whose favour I should intervene. Then it was the stranger in the overcoat's turn to pass by me. He rushed into his Carden. The little car did a perfect ninety-degree turn and set off in pursuit of the man in flight.

I rushed to the spot where the colonel and his wife lay in agony. Fantin had lost consciousness, his hair sticky from a thin trickle of blood above the right ear. He moved feebly, groaning the while; a revolver lay a few centimetres from his hand. On the other hand, Mme de Larsaudière did not move at all: a bullet had got her in the throat. You could see a dark stain spreading over her chest. I looked for the little suitcase the colonel was carrying as well as for the envelope. One of the two men had taken everything.

It would have been foolish to stay on the spot any longer. The little cottages must have been buzzing with questions about the gunshots and all the comings and goings of cars... Somebody would soon come out to take care of Fantin before he froze!

The Packard was much more difficult to manoeuvre than the Carden. First of all I had to get out of the narrow corridor formed by the shelter and a fence, without rubbing against it, then turn full lock twice over to get back in the direction of the road. There were no crossroads before Tremblay-lès-Gonesse. I had a good chance of catching up with the rest of the convoy by burning rubber.

The two others weren't stopping to play games. I passed the sign for the parish of Tremblay-lès-Gonesse without having seen their rear lights. A series of little streets, farm entrances, a string of workers' allotments passed by, so that I had to slow down to make sure the people I was chasing hadn't turned down any of them.

I went round the town square in second and nearly crashed into a royal milestone placed right on the edge of the pavement. It was strange: the original fleur-de-lys on top of the block of stone had been replaced by a Phrygian bonnet. The peasants must have had it up to the hilt before '89 for them to take their revenge even on highway signs!

The beam of my lights revealed a bronze statue of a soldier who seemed to be pointing out the direction of the main road with his finger. I let myself be convinced.

The well-surfaced road sloped gently down for about two kilometres towards the village of Villepinte. Some bare poplar trees edged the road, one planted every twenty-five metres. Quite a wall. I speeded up but the vibrations from the paving-stones wouldn't let me go any faster than ninety.

Every now and then, gusts of wind blew over the sickening smell of a river of effluent which ran along the road. The only answer was to breathe in small gasps, which didn't save me from taking in more than enough. I left the cemetery on the right, and the massive silhouette of the sanatorium stood out against the skyline. Close by there, tiny points of light shone out before disappearing. It could only be them.

They were still too far ahead for me to be able to catch them up before they went into the village. I found myself in the same position as at Tremblay, with four possible choices of direction. La Croix-l'Aumône, Gonesse, Le Bel-Air, Aulnay? No bronze soldier this time to save my bacon…

The square was empty, all the cafés had closed their shutters. I stopped in front of the hospital gate to give myself time to think. That's when I noticed an old man sitting on a bench, impervious to the cold. He was smoking his pipe with his gaze fixed on me. I came up and lowered my window.

'Good evening.'

He felt it was sufficient to give a nod of the head while expelling a puff of smoke.

'Have you by any chance seen two cars go by? I was part of the convoy but I lost sight of them in the dark…'

He pulled the pipe out of his mouth and with the back of his hand wiped away the thin string of saliva that, momentarily, attached it to his lips.

'They went straight ahead… In the Pont du Marais area… If I were in your shoes, I'd leave my car here. The road stops fifty metres further on… A real mess… They've never done anything to straighten it out…'

And that was putting it mildly! Hundreds of carts must trundle down this road over the course of the year. Their wheels had left deep ruts along which the Packard drove as if on rails. I skirted around the block of houses several times before finding the Citroën parked in a little courtyard in front of an unpretentious villa. I got out to examine inside the car. Dark brown stains were smeared over the front seat, on the driver's side. I didn't bother to try it on my fingers: the sickening smell of blood filled the interior. I slid out my Webley for the second time that evening. The other car, the Carden, had disappeared. Unless, that is, it was parked somewhere in the shadow and its owner was just about to fill me full of lead. Mentally, I warned him not to waste his first shot. I didn't make a gift of myself when it came to saving my skin.

I crossed the courtyard. I bounded up the stairs leading to the front door of the villa, every sense on the alert. A shiver ran down my back. I resisted the overwhelming desire to turn around, gun at the ready. I had to tell myself: there is no one. NO ONE. Otherwise you're finished; you can't go on without jumping at every leaf that falls...

I pushed open the door with my knee. It opened creakily. A long corridor divided the space into two equal parts, crossed at the far end by a thin line of light. I flattened up against the wall on my right, arm held out stiffly in readiness, and began to slide silently down to the end of the corridor. When I banged my forehead against the door-frame, I closed my eyes for a fraction of a second, and held my breath to increase my concentration before launching myself into the room. I scanned the room methodically with my Webley.

It was clear I was taking too much trouble: the gentleman in the glasses had no chance of giving grief to anyone any more.

He hadn't had time to take off his coat, the other guy must have been following close behind. His hideous-looking body lay on the floor. He had been hit by two bullets, the first one in his arm, between the left shoulder and the elbow. That wound explained the bloodstains in the car. The second bullet had been enough to kill him on the spot: you don't blow away half of someone's skull with impunity!

He had had every intention of defending himself before dying, as a pistol lay near his good arm among some linen that had fallen out of a drawer. I skirted round the body, my attention caught by the suitcase belonging to Colonel Fantin which had been left open on the bed. Empty. Bundles of notes were scattered on the eiderdown as if the stranger had thrown them down out of pique. Other bundles littered the ground, some of them soaked in blood. It couldn't be far off the 100,000 francs of the ransom money. I turned the house over to try and find the envelope, without any luck. Before leaving I picked up the dead man's pistol; it was a Ruby, one of those rubbishy Spanish guns that blow up in your face half the time! At one point that was all they were issuing to us, as if the Germans weren't causing enough havoc among our ranks...

I looked at the chamber: not a bullet missing.

It wasn't too difficult to recreate the scene: after the meeting at Roissy-en-France, the blackmailer, wounded, had come back to shelter at his house, intending to put the envelope and Fantin's suitcase in a safe place. The third man, who had crossed my path, concealed from head to foot by his oversize coat, had followed him here.

The first guy must have made the mistake of going to Roissy unarmed. His first thought had been to run to his bedroom to try and get the Ruby. His murderer didn't give him the time to get that far... One bullet to rub him out, for good. He had picked up the envelope and had stuffed his pockets full of notes without making the mistake of taking the suitcase, sticky with blood spilt on the journey.

I went out again after I had taken care to wipe all the objects that I had touched. The area still seemed as quiet as when

I had come. No one seemed to have heard the gunfire nor the comings and goings of cars. Or else the nearness of the sanatorium had a pernicious influence on the locals: it became a habit to play dead.

As I went past the town hall once again, the old man was still sat upon his bench with his back to the sanatorium. I pretended not to see him, but when I passed him, he took his pipe out of his mouth and waved me goodbye in a way I would rather he hadn't.

I was just crossing the fortifications at the gate of La Villette when the clock struck eleven. I didn't have the energy to go out of my way to put the car in the garage... In the bedroom, Irène had fallen asleep still clothed, not even under the cover. I can't have been looking my best for, still only half-awake, she warmed my face with her hot hands and pulled me towards her. Giving a little yawn, she looked at me through her damp lashes.

'Things don't seem to be going too well... Don't tell me you've been playing pilots again!'

I fell on to the bed and covered my head with the eiderdown. I gave up the struggle against the immense fatigue that, suddenly, pinned me down. It was nothing to do with being tired but more with the aching feeling that I couldn't grasp anything about this story, I had nothing in my hands but useless shreds. A wave of despondency ran over me with a sudden chill. I would not let myself be sucked down. I stood up again.

'I'm a bit hungry. Is there anything left?'

'Would you like me to make you a ham omelette?'

I smiled as I remembered it was my day to do the cooking.

'Why are you laughing? What did I say?'

'Nothing... I was just remembering that Colonel Fantin

offered me the same thing that day he rang me up in such a mess ... An omelette! Tonight was total carnage!'

She answered me while she was breaking the eggs on the side of the sink.

'We can save buying a paper; you can read it in your face. At least you haven't been hurt, have you?'

'Not me ... Fantin's wife has been killed as well as the blackmailer.'

'Who was he?'

'I've no idea ... I didn't hang around the area. A bloke about fifty years old, going bald with round glasses ... He lives at Villepinte, not far from the sanatorium ...'

'I wasn't mistaken: I was convinced she'd get herself bumped off! Was it your colonel?'

Since the beginning Irène had settled on this hypothesis. As far as she was concerned Fantin was trying to get rid of his wife.

'It's impossible to tell how it happened! As the handover was taking place Fantin and his wife were facing the man with glasses. I was hiding, further up the road. Between us there was another guy who wasn't listed in the programme ... Just as everything was gently unfolding, he jumped the group with a pistol in his hand. I heard two shots. Mme de Larsaudière fell almost immediately. The second bullet must have got the blackmailer in the arm. Fantin had a blow from the butt of a gun. He was out for the count when I got a bit closer.'

'What did he say when he came to?'

'You don't think I was going to wait for the cops to come! No one knows I've set foot in Roissy this evening. Not even Fantin. I disappeared. The guy in glasses had taken advantage of the general confusion to get away with the money and the papers. With the stranger hot on his heels … I followed their trail as far as Villepinte, too late by a hair's breadth: just enough to be left high and dry. One extra body … As you might guess, the envelope had disappeared. Two violent deaths in the same neck of the woods; that'll cause a stir! I'd better lie low for a few days.'

'But you're not guilty of anything … And anyway if no one's seen you, we'll make up an alibi. No?'

'Oh shit! To be quite accurate: I asked someone the way, in the hamlet. You can't think of everything all the time …'

'That doesn't matter. It'll be his word against yours. Is there anything else? Truthfully …'

'You should listen to yourself sometimes! For the last five minutes you've been treating me as if I was a murderer on the run. I've just got away from an ambush and you're casting doubt on me … It won't hold up: the car is covered in mud. I went over a few dilapidated roads before getting to the villa. The cops aren't stupid, they'll quickly work out where the car's been!'

Irène didn't let this put her off. She tipped the beaten eggs into the bubbling fat.

'Take your time eating. Then, we can go to the canal bank to wash it down … If the cops follow the trail as far as you, they might not let go!'

I suspected she was right. The other solution was to find some thick-headed commissioner and to tell him my story. The mystery of the Man in the Dark Overcoat! It wasn't hard to guess what I'd get out of a civic act noble enough to appeal to shop-girls: nothing but blows and headaches!

I slid the omelette on to a plate, then I got a cold beer off the window-ledge of the kitchen.

Irène got dressed. She sprayed herself with perfume and the scent blended with the taste in my mouth. A sweet treat.

'You smell nice. Have you just bought it?'

'No, it's only Eau de Louvain, that's all.'

It took me a few seconds to register.

'Can't you call it Eau de Cologne like everyone else!'

'No! Eau de Louvain ... When they censored all the German names, at the end of 1914, that was all you heard: "A bottle of Eau de Louvain, please, a big one." "Oh, how beautiful your Alsatian is"...'

She stopped simpering, with pouting lips.

'It was difficult enough for me to remember that my metro stop was now called Jaurès instead of Allemagne. Without taking into account the miracles of self-control needed to avoid ordering Prussian blue or Frankfurt sausages! Do you remember, if you had a slip of the tongue, you were fucked, you were denounced as a German spy. Now we have to do an about face, at the drop of a hat! No! I'm going to go on using Eau de Louvain for as long as I want!'

I couldn't decide if this sudden fit of temper was genuine or put on. I often felt this was part of a game, a playful provocation. To cut it short, I went up to her from behind and kissed her at the fold between her ear and her neck. I wanted her straight away and tried to lead her into the bedroom. She resisted.

'Later, please ... Don't you think it's more important to take care of the car? Especially as I've got some news ...'

The magic words: I let her go.

'Some news? To do with the Fantin affair?'

She looked me up and down, smiling ironically.

'You don't know what you want more. Which are you going to choose, the information or me?'

'Stop your fooling around! If you like we could combine the two subjects, you can tell me everything in bed...'

She moved towards the door of the flat.

'No, while we're washing off the mud... I haven't been wasting my time this afternoon. I've become an expert in the market in pig meat. Don't get angry, I'm not referring to you!'

The cops didn't like roaming around the coal-loading area on the Quai de la Marne after nightfall. The occasional lamp-post illuminated the corner-shop windows with a faded light. The cops weren't the only ones to avoid the area. It was deserted. Irène used a saucepan to take water out of the canal while I washed the bodywork and the tyres. A car went by in the distance and slowed down; I made out the glow of a cigarette behind the windscreen, the sight of us held the occupants' attention for a few seconds. They moved on; with a bit of patience one could come across something even more unusual than a couple washing their car at midnight, on the edge of the Ourcq.

'Come on then, tell me your secrets...'

She put her saucepan down on the running board.

'OK, if you promise not to come near me... Here we go: the Darsac cognacs have a minority share in Clairmont Tinned Foods. Ten per cent. And the cognac is Madame...'

'It was! Soon the colonel will pocket everything: the casks plus 10 per cent of the tins... How did you manage to dig out such information so quickly! It would have taken me two days!'

'I try to be nice. It's as easy as that. Sure, we have access by law to the decisions of annual general meetings, but you can also be nice to the clerical administration. Smile at the archivist at the Chamber of Commerce next time you go. Who knows?'

'I'd already thought of that, but his moustache would put me off! So the Fantins are in this up to their necks?'

'No, it's not as simple as that. You don't have control of the board with 10 per cent. Anyway we're not talking about monkey business: the transactions over pig meat are dubious but they're not yet under legal scrutiny. I doubt whether it'll ever come to that. The Minister of Supply should have been more vigilant. Especially as he's not unconnected: he belongs to the Clairmont family. By marriage.'

I stopped rubbing the front bumper.

'The worst of it all is that you really imagine that you're making my job easier by giving me such information! Can you see me setting off to track down a corrupt minister who's made a fortune out of shady deals involving thousands of tons of pig meat! I'm not that kind of heavyweight...'

'Come on, don't underestimate yourself. In the meantime, you should ask your American friend, Bob, what he's playing at!'

'Bob's got nothing to do with this! He takes care of the depot at Pleyel. There are no perishable foodstuffs there.'

She picked up the saucepan again and bent down to refill it in the canal.

'Then explain to me what he was doing at the Clairmont factory at the Porte de Pantin this afternoon. I took a trip down there to have a look at the mess... I saw him conferring with a gang of suits. It looked important. Does he take tourists round the abattoirs?'

'You're quite sure it was Bob?'

'Yes, without a shadow of doubt. I don't know anyone else

who would dare wear those dreadful blue trousers covered in stitching! Apart from you, of course…'

I grabbed the container from her hands and threw the contents violently on the bodywork.

'Get in, I want to sort things out.'

The car left the quay with the engine firing irregularly before it settled into its usual rhythm. The fine layer of soot covering the pavement was blown up by gusts of wind. With the rain it found its way into the tiniest cracks: invisible particles of coal crunched under our teeth.

Down the boulevards, at the cabaret doors, not a single bouncer remembered having seen Bob. Yeah, he'd been spotted the day before, towing behind him half-a-dozen rich Brazilians.

I was about to give up when a doorman at the Cigale discreetly told me that he was expecting him at two in the morning, for dinner with a bunch of tourists. I didn't have the patience to stick around, worrying myself to death. Irène offered to stake the place out while I combed the last night-clubs, over by Barbès Rochechouart.

I got through a long fifteen minutes this way before coming back to Pigalle. I came across him at the top of the Rue Fontaine just as he was coming out of the Sengra, a neo-realist night spot that featured fat women.

The Brazilians had been drinking. Without the support of their starched shirts, not one of them would have been able to stay on his feet! They greeted me with joy when they realized that I was a mate of their guide. Bob greeted me with a big smile. Things seemed set to go well.

'So, René, you're turning into a night-bird? Don't tell me you're looking for me?'

I wasn't in the mood to smile back at him. He quickly noticed that I was gritting my teeth and put on a serious expression.

'That's exactly it, I was looking for you ... Are you surprised?'

'Yes, especially at this time ... It's been a fair while since you've been hanging around Montmartre so late.'

I lowered my voice.

'Can we have a quiet chat without your herd hanging around?'

'Up yours! They may be drunk but they understand French ... Don't interfere with my work!'

I pulled him over to one side, nearly down to the corner of the Douai Road. The Brazilians tried to go back into the cabaret; the fat women were attracting a lot of trade. Bob leant up against the frame of a door in the mews.

'So? What do you want from me then? It must be serious for you to be up and about in the middle of the night.'

'We might as well put our cards on the table: are you involved with Clairmont Tinned Foods and their shady deals in rotting pig meat? Yes or no, I'm in a hurry!'

'Since when did you get interested? That meat comes from the USA, Chicago to be precise. I suppose you know that?'

'Yes, that doesn't change anything.'

'On the contrary ... The negotiators speak American. I'm just the go-between for the two parties. A kind of interpreter.'

He suddenly seemed to be more ill at ease. Irène was right: the bastard was playing the two sides off against each other.

'You won't get out of it that easily, Bob. You remember last week, when I was hot on the trail of Mme de Larsaudière ...'

'Yes, I remember. You wanted me to listen to what people were saying about her. I was on the level with you...'

'Not quite. You forgot to tell me that you were working for the Fantin family as well... I think that makes a difference! They have shares in Clairmont. So?'

Bob bent his head, and combed back a lock of hair with his fingers.

'I'm not going to tell the story of my life to the whole world! Yes, I know your colonel. We met by chance... An American who was going home tipped me off about the salt meat. I meet all the big shots in the international market, people in the Ministry of Supply and people from Clairmont at Pleyel from time to time... They're all in the business... The colonel probably noticed that I made out all right... He was looking for a detective for some private business... A matter of honour. He needed an ace. I gave him your name.'

'That's very kind of you, but I had no intention of taking on a manager! Don't expect to get a commission!'

'Stop getting at me, René. I put a top-class client your way, on a plate, and all you can do is get mad at me! He's behaved badly, that must be it... Has he refused to pay you?'

'No, in some way, I'd have preferred that! Why didn't you warn me your client was coming? One phone call...'

'He didn't want me to, so I didn't bother. Besides, can you imagine a colonel introducing himself by saying: "I've been recommended to see you by Bob, the gigolo of Montmartre!" It would have looked bad.'

His explanations didn't hold water. I'd have been prepared to swallow them from anyone except Bob. There was no way he would have kept secret a coup like that... 'How much did he pay you not to tell me anything?'

'It's no fun with you, René, you know everything, you know my every weak spot...'

'How much?'

'Fifty francs to be discreet. It's not a lot, I must have been feeling generous that day!'

'He must have topped it up a good bit to get you to put me on his wife's trail, Mme de Larsaudière, at the Bois?'

Bob was clearly shaken. I had thrown the question out without thinking too much about where it might lead.

'Who gave you a sniff of this set-up?'

'I'm the one asking the questions, Bob. I want to know what's the price of friendship to you? Tell me!'

'The same thing; 50 francs. What are you trying to dig up? Big words like betrayal, it sounds good... The fact is, the colonel needed to catch her red-handed in order to get a divorce without any scandal. He wasn't going to arrange a police raid on the night-club. That would have ruined his family reputation for at least ten generations... Whereas a private eye could have given evidence of his wife's immoral conduct without anything having to come out in public. I've made 100 francs even though I know it stinks; you've already done a good week's work on ground that had been prepared for you... Surely you've had the opportunity to pocket dirtier money than that! Come on, stop sulking; you're still sore at me for that doing over you got from the pilots! You'd better get over it, there'll be more!'

'Indeed, that's what I fear. I hope for your sake that you're not more involved than that in Fantin's business.'

'Why? Is there more shit?'

I was within a whisker of saying to him: 'Because now there are two stiffs laid out.' I just managed to hold myself back. No one knew anything about it and Bob shouldn't know that I had been around Villepinte earlier in the evening. Might as well leave him a big surprise to read about in the morning paper.

I went back to the Cigale to relieve Irène from the bar. I was more miserable than I'd been for a long time. She looked at me questioningly.

'Yeah, Bob was in the know.'

She hugged me tight until we got home, without saying anything. My gaze fixed on the cobbles, a metre in front of the bonnet, I caught myself thinking that it was better to have two bodies to deal with than to lose a friend…

Both had happened to me at the same time!

CHAPTER 8

The next day I got up very early. The stove had gone out in the night and the inside of the windows was misted up. I put on a jacket while I lit the stove. There's nothing worse than starting the day feeling damp and cold.

The washing-up was piled up in the sink, and my spirits sank. I went down to the Café des Travailleurs, the meeting-place for all the mechanics who repaired anything on wheels. Everyone involved in the goods market met up there. Usually you couldn't hear yourself speak but early in the morning the guys were quiet, still recovering from yesterday's activity.

I ordered a coffee which the bartender gave me between a glass of red and a cognac.

His wife sold cigarettes and the morning papers at the other end of the counter. They didn't talk to each other; you couldn't get anything from one by asking the other. You got used to it.

I went to buy *Le Matin*, expecting to see Fantin's name splashed across the front page. I was disappointed. There was plenty of coverage of military men on page one, but no mention of mine!

In fact, the President of the Council had yesterday received a deputation of five hundred men blinded in the war. On this occasion General Maunoury, 'Conqueror of the Ourcq', had seen himself (the journalist had fallen for the unfortunate choice of words) raised to the rank of 'First Blind Man of France'.

A worker tossing down his beer before going back to work glanced at the headline and nudged me.

'For once, they're right! A general king of the blind ... we've been telling them that for years ... Only we had to pay the price, with a skinful of bullets!'

I nodded my head in agreement. I leafed through the rag until I came to the news in brief. Last night's two deaths were written about separately, in two short articles. First I read the one about Fantin's wife.

BRUTAL ATTACK IN SEINE-ET-OISE
Mme de Larsaudière is killed.

At about nine o'clock last night, as they were driving between Roissy-en-France and Tremblay-lès-Gonesse, the car driven by Mme de Larsaudière and in which her husband Colonel Fantin de Larsaudière was travelling was attacked by several thugs. Colonel Fantin, who is well known for his bravery since his regiment, the 296th, received the most awards for daring action during the war, resisted the attackers fiercely.

The latter then used their firearms. In a confused exchange of fire, Mme de Larsaudière was fatally wounded while Colonel Fantin received a head wound.

This brutal attack on one of the most well-known personages of the day can be linked with other crimes of the same sort which now, alas, appear all too frequently on our pages.

> The turbulence arising from the recent conflict with Germany has not miraculously ended on Armistice Day. Criminal statistics show a rise in crime attributable to demobbed soldiers who are unable to reinsert themselves into society. There are also very many fatherless young men according to statistics released by the police authorities.
>
> May we remind you that Mme de Larsaudière, née Darsac, was head of Cognac Darsac and that she was honorary President of the Friendly Society for the Children of Deceased Officers.
>
> According to the latest information available to us, the police are concentrating their enquiries among the numerous criminal elements of that area of Seine-et-Oise. It has to be remembered that large 'colonies' of Parisian criminals have moved to Aulnay, Villepinte or Blanc-Mesnil after a sentence which refused them the right to live in the department of the Seine. By living just outside the forbidden department, they are able to enter to commit crimes at will.

The Colonel had acted quickly: *Le Matin* had already published, on the following page in the Diary section, the traditional announcement paid for by the family.

Colonel François Fantin de Larsaudière
Luce Fantin de Larsaudière
announce with great sorrow
the tragic death of their wife and mother
Amélie Fantin de Larsaudière
née Darsac.

A second similar announcement followed, this time from the Darsac family and the group of companies.

The third, and most unexpected, bore the signature of M. Danrémont, President and Director-General of Clairmont Tinned Foods.

The corpse in glasses in the villa at Villepinte did not get so much attention. His link with posterity was concluded with a few lines:

> MURDER AT VILLEPINTE
> M. Roger Fauge, a nurse at the sanatorium in Villepinte, was found dead by one of his neighbours who was worried when he found the light on and the door open early in the morning. The police found the body of M. Fauge, with several bullet holes, in the bedroom of the villa, along with 10,000 francs. According to people in the neighbourhood the victim led a quiet life. The police are working on the hypothesis that there was a family quarrel which ended badly.

I refolded the paper.

'Landlord! A whisky!'

'I don't have such a thing. On the other hand, I can offer you an authentic calva. It hasn't had to go through Bercy. Try a sniff!'

I let myself be tempted. The mixture reached my stomach quicker than a stew on wheels, when it's time to eat and you're hungry.

The alcohol warmed up and the fumes began to soothe my nerves.

Despite the intervention, I couldn't bring myself to believe that the cops in Seine-et-Oise were so stupid . . . A fantasy about brigands in the Forêt de Bondy was all right for sending shivers around the Old Veterans, at the end of a charity dinner. They could have invented something better! The yarn about the nurse was even more ridiculous . . . As they say in journalism, the bigger the lie, the better it goes down.

THE DOC HAD A DOUBLE LIFE: HE SAVED THEM BY DAY AND KILLED THEM BY NIGHT!

They could take me on as a headliner at *Le Matin*; I was more than ready. A calva to start with and I could keep going till nightfall.

I went home, lost in thought. Obviously they were trying to disassociate the two events to the point of dividing by ten the sum of money found with Roger Fauge . . . Ten thousand francs, it was serious family business. A hundred thousand, their story no longer held water!

Irène was washing herself, naked in front of the mirror, one foot on the edge of the sink. I squeezed myself against her back and spread my hands across her breasts. 'You're mad! Your hands are frozen!'

She realized that just touching her released powerful kinetic forces and let herself be carried over to the bed, with one leg still soapy. She wrapped herself in a sheet to put on a record by the Witheman sextet, 'Wang Wang Blues', without giving a thought to where it came from. I frowned.

'Oh no! Not that song! I'm going to throw out that whole collection. I can't listen to a single one of those records without the first note reminding me that they were given to me by that shit Bob…'

With the tip of her toe, Irène lifted up the pile of clothes that I had hastily thrown off.

'You're less picky about the "jeans" and the aviator's jacket! Aren't you bothered about wearing those? Even though they come from the same source.'

'I agree. You're right. Parcel up the records and the clothes. We'll give them to the poor, to wish them a Happy New Year.'

'And the stock of bourbon?'

'Leave that where it is. I'll keep it; to help me forget…'

Sex at dusk leaves you blue; sex at dawn, you're in a stew.

I felt like getting dressed in civvies: flannel trousers, thick cotton jacket. Just as I was setting off for Aulnay I was stopped in my tracks by the telephone ringing. I didn't recognize the voice at first.

'Hello, is this the Griffon office?'

'Yes. René Griffon speaking. At your service.'

'Inspector Aubry of the Paris PJ. I'm very pleased to find you at home…'

It wasn't enough that he should bother me; he also felt he could be very patronizing. Yet I didn't have a special relationship with the PJ. Probably the cops in the area barely knew I existed. There are some private eyes who spend their whole time in the police department; granted, there are some things that can be sorted out that way… guys who thought they were cops 'come in from the cold' with the idea that they were doing the same job, just one step down the ladder. Idiots! In fact they were taken for a ride.

I wanted him to introduce himself.

'You must be mistaken, I don't know any Inspector Aubry.'

My caller laughed. Five little ha-has strung together like pearls.

'Clément Aubry! I grant you, I wasn't an inspector then ... I've gone up in the ranks ...'

It was enough to make you despair! Especially as in the police, as in the army, principles and intelligence don't breed as fast as stripes.

'Fancy that! It must be at least a year ...'

'Just about, yes. I'm covering the Fantin affair ...'

He took me by surprise. I couldn't understand why the Paris PJ should be involved with the affair in Roissy. I pretended ignorance in order to gain time.

'What Fantin affair?'

'Haven't you read the papers?'

'No, I've just got up. I was stopped short by your phone call just as I was going downstairs to get the bread. Has something happened to the gentleman?'

'Not really; let's just say a terrible headache! It's more a question of his wife ... A bullet in the throat. A powerful remedy for tonsilitis! I would like to ask you a couple of questions. If you can come by this morning, I'll be in room 205. Agreed?'

He was asking my opinion for form's sake; his question rang out like an order.

'OK. I'll come. Just give me time to snatch a coffee.'

I hung up but kept my hand on the receiver, not sure what to do. Irène was looking at me.

'Was it the colonel?'

'No, the cops. I should have known, they're not as stupid as they seem. Seems they're even learning how to drive ... They've put the investigation into the hands of the PJ Inspector Aubry to sort things out; a piece of shit on the make!'

'Why, do you know him?'

I buried my nose in the paper so that I wouldn't have to reply. Know him, that would be putting it strongly. Aubry and I had met in '19, in the spring, when I was just getting my agency off the ground. To be honest I was thrashing around badly, the job was new to me ... Before the war I'd had a go at all kinds of work, mechanic, printer, newsagent at a kiosk in the Rue Lafayette, and even actor for a day. I had good memories of that one: I played a fisherman casting his line. I never saw the end product, it came out when I was involved in an international epic near Verdun ... It was a film by Georges Leblond, *Nadia the Weird*.

A friend had put me in touch with Aubry. According to him, he was willing to teach me the tricks of the trade: unobtrusive shadowing, making contact, the psychology ...

At that time Aubry was working for the War Ministry and was very discreet about how he spent his time. I was vaguely aware that he was sent on missions to Switzerland, every two or three months. His orders there were to hang around the cafés where the French gathered and to make friends with the clientele.

I have to explain that several thousand soldiers had taken refuge in Geneva and Berne, to escape the slaughter. The flow had gathered momentum in April 1917 after the absurd offensive on Nivelle. As soon as he ferreted out a deserter, Aubry would get him drunk and take him back, at the end of the day, to the French border-post ... With a court martial at journey's end.

It wasn't surprising that he got promoted now that the

Government was easing up on the practice. There would be an amnesty decreed soon, supposedly for the 'missing soldiers' but really so that everyone would forget to ask too many questions.

We had talked business three evenings on the trot, at my place. I managed to get the maximum information out of him without giving anything in return, then goodbye!

There are some relationships that have the same effect on you as strawberries: you want them and then they bring you out in a rash!

Aubry hadn't changed. He'd barely put on weight as he grew in importance. He made an effort to be friendly right from the start by putting all his cards on the table.

'We know that Colonel Fantin was using your services. Some deplorable blackmail, most probably. Where had you got to in your enquiries?'

'How long have you known that?'

Aubry busied himself lighting a cigarette. My question brought a smile to his lips.

'Since last night. Some peasants heard the gunfire... I tried to get hold of you round about midnight... But you're too busy to stay at home.'

He tried to act casual, to avoid any innuendo. To win my confidence while examining my reactions minutely. He wasn't passing on all this information to prove he trusted me, but just the opposite, to put me off my guard!

I might as well give him a reply in kind. With discretion.

'I read the newspapers coming over here. They've fallen for the bait... The headlines blame it all on wandering bands of soldiers.'

'We decide on the target. They have to take our word... As long as we have no idea of what exactly is going on in this business, we have orders to protect Colonel Fantin's reputation. An arrest in the full glare of publicity is out of the question when we're dealing with the private life of a national hero. It would have a terrible effect on the general public. We just don't need something so idiotic at present. There are strikes breaking out all over the place, we're not going to fan the flames... Do you get the drift of my meaning?' The message was clear. On the side, I was trying to decode what was being hinted at.

'I'm not a fool. I've got to keep my trap shut, isn't that it?'

Inspector Aubry came round to the front of his desk to slap me on the shoulder.

'You've got it. Just be a bit discreet, we're not asking for anything more. Anyway, where had you got to?'

'Not very far... I was well paid and I was trying to spin the job out. The colonel must have figured that out. He fired me yesterday, on the phone. My secretary managed to negotiate a week's salary, as notice...'

'I don't want to know everything that happens in your firm. Had you discovered something?'

'I guess his wife cuckolded him at the least temptation. As soon as some guy took a sniff, she jumped on him! I was given the job, I suppose, to pinpoint which one of this happy band was taking advantage of the situation to get some pocket-money out of the husband. Nothing very magical about it... An old story. I was in no hurry to get to the bottom of it only to have to scrape around for another client who paid 100 francs a day!'

Aubry whistled with admiration.

'One hundred francs! You don't pull any punches...'

'He's got plenty of money. In the end, just the simple fact of my appearance around the colonel and his wife was enough to get the blackmailer to rush things. Wouldn't you agree?'

'It's not bad, Griffon… But you've still got a way to go. Colonel Fantin has certainly used you to flush the wolf out of the undergrowth. If it turns out to be true, you'll have earned your commission: mission accomplished. Seeing what happened, he made one big mistake: not keeping you around to carry out the exchange. According to the first information we have, the colonel had an appointment with his blackmailer in Roissy-en-France, at about nine o'clock in the evening. He rarely drove, so his wife took the wheel.'

'Isn't that surprising?'

'What should I be surprised at, Griffon?'

'That the wife doesn't blink at meeting her ex-lover with her husband…'

'No, I've seen worse things… Couples often decide to put up a united front against something that threatens them more than their differences. Just as the exchange was taking place, things got out of hand. The colonel gave the money, 10,000 francs, to the unknown man. The other was going to give him letters written by Mme de Larsaudière in exchange, when a third man with a gun intervened. The colonel, feeling threatened, wanted to defend himself. He waved a gun. The assailant, who must have been taken by surprise by this resistance, let off several gunshots. The colonel doesn't remember much; he was knocked out just after the exchange of fire. The locals found him at ten past nine, unconscious, next to his wife's body.'

'Who told you about these letters?'

'The colonel, this morning… Why?'

I pretended not to attach too much importance to this detail.

'Nothing... I felt sure it was something like this... What's your conclusion?'

He folded his arms across his chest, looking well satisfied.

'It's self-evident! It's child's play and only an old soldier would let himself be taken in... The blackmailer set up an ambush in two stages: first he picks up the money from the blackmail then one of his mates comes out of the shadows to scare the shit out of everyone in the middle of the exchange. Benefits all round. You can take off to come back another day! That's how things should have happened... But there was a hiccup. The colonel was a little bit suspicious. Usually, people lose their nerve in front of the barrel of a gun. He didn't. He confronted it, like a hero.'

'You tell the story as if you were there...'

I thought he might have let slip a smile. Nothing. He continued:

'One assumes that the agreement between the two accomplices fell apart when it came to sharing out the goods... We found the body of one of them at a villa in Villepinte. The money too, 10,000 francs, well almost all of it. The murderer must have decided not to take it, it was covered in blood...'

He was sticking to the story of 10,000 francs as well. I'd have been surprised if he thought a simple case of misplaced sex was worth 100,000 francs... Aubry must know a bit more about the ramifications of the Fantin and Darsac families!

'Do you know the dead man's name?'

I asked the question automatically; I could see myself still reading the article, in the Café des Travailleurs.

'Yes, he was a nurse at the sanatorium in Villepinte, Roger Fauge. We've got his photo; he doesn't seem at all like a lady's man … I know you'll tell me that you've only got to look at Landru's mug to know that anyone can get in with the ladies! Anyway, there's only one left to ferret out …'

He said these last words looking me directly in the eyes. There was a silence, then he went on.

'It shouldn't be long, in my opinion. A guy who panics to the point of leaving all the money behind as a clue can't go very far. Ten thousand francs! You wouldn't have made a blunder like that! Two murders with not a bean to show for it … Do you have any idea who this guy might be, Griffon?'

For one fleeting moment I thought that the old guy taking the air outside the sanatorium, the night before, must have talked. Besides, I had the same outline as the missing link!

If he had him as a witness, Aubry, with the help of the PJ, would have no trouble in reconstructing my mad evening: the stake-out at Roissy-en-France, the chase through Tremblay-lès-Gonesse, my call at Roger Fauge's house …

When you added it all up, I had very little in my defence: a Carden and a profile seen at night. No one could believe a story straight out of a cheap thriller. I pretended to show no great concern when I replied.

'No, I don't know what kind of crackpot would have taken on a plan with so many double-crosses. You'd better have a prowl round the corridors of the sanatorium, it might have been a joke set up by some of the nurses that went sour …'

'Thanks for the tip. Luckily policemen's gags are more innocent … In any case, Fantin's statement has been confirmed so far. We found the tracks of the third man's car. He was parked behind a bus shelter. A big car. We're going to try and get prints of the marks left by the tyres ...'

I began to feel ill at ease. Not only was this bastard playing on my nerves, but he seemed to take great pleasure in it. I swallowed hard before speaking.

'Is it the same method as for taking fingerprints?'

'Let's not exaggerate. The technique is brand-new; we've nothing to lose by giving it a go.'

'You think you'll be able to trace the car this way?'

'There's a small chance ... Unfortunately the ground is frozen at the moment. The laboratory will do all it can. No promises, you always end up being disappointed!'

I unclenched my jaw and fists. It was impossible to tell what was true or false in everything he was telling me. I stood up.

'Do you need me for anything else?'

He made do with a shake of the head to show that he didn't. He changed his mind as I was closing the door.

'By the way ... A formality ... Where were you that night when I rang you at home?'

I had been expecting this question since the interview began. I relaxed completely when I heard it. The roles became clearer. He didn't see me smile. I had my back to him, my face against the door-jamb.

'In Montmartre, with a friend, Irène. We called in at a few night-clubs, the Sengra on the Rue Fontaine and the Cigale, on the boulevard ... Why?'

He muttered:

'Nothing, nothing. Just routine. Bye.'

I left the Cité as soon as possible to dive into the first bar I came across: a watering hole for all the employees of the police headquarters. They drank lemonade or coffee while telling each other the latest sordid gossip on the jostling at the top of the Central Police Department. That's how the *esprit de corps* gets reinforced!

I tried to think things over while I sipped a stale double bourbon. It wasn't my day for sure. There was only one thing missing for the picture to become catastrophic: that Aubry should lay his hands on the old man with the pipe...

I needed to move things along. The net was getting tighter every minute. More than one detail of Aubry's story didn't fit with my perception of the exchange. Colonel Fantin was the key to the mystery. Of course, the unknown man in the overcoat as well, but it wasn't even worth thinking about catching him quickly... First I had to see Fantin and do a bit of probing to see what traps Aubry had laid for me or if he was truly repeating the colonel's statements.

I decided to take the road to Aulnay; this was becoming a habit. To vary things, I left by the Porte de Pantin and Drancy.

CHAPTER 9

In fact, this route was shorter. I only realized when my job was coming to an end! I did the journey in record time. I would have done even better if I hadn't been held up by a clash between a police squad and Bolshevik demonstrators.

The bunch of young workers, ten at the most, were covering all the walls they could find with strident posters, in red, white and black. The same slogan was written on them all:

'FREE TILLON AND MARTY'
'LONG LIVE LENIN'

You saw a lot of these posters around, ever since the military tribunal at Brest had given Charles Tillon a five-year prison sentence. The week before Christmas. He was accused of having refused to fight against Soviet troops. André Marty, the son of a communard, had been rotting between four walls for almost a year now for inciting troops to mutiny.

Tens of other sailors from the *Guichen*, the *France*, the *Jean-Bart* and the *Waldeck-Rousseau* were breaking stones under threat of a thrashing at Dar el-Hamri, in Morocco, or else they were draining the marshes around Kenitra. The factory-owners had long been demanding a return to normality.

The Bolshies, as were called the members of the Communist International who were agitating strongly in the midst of the Socialist Party, had seized on the examples of Marty and Tillon, to set up a particularly aggressive campaign. They were gaining support in the suburbs.

I was about to go round the group when a Renault lorry, like those which used to go to the front, shot out from the right and came to a halt across the road. The doors opened on all sides, spilling out a swarm of policemen, their caps pulled down on their heads, their cloaks dancing to the rhythm of the charge. Their batons looked like white stains against their uniforms.

The encircling movement was carried out like a parade-ground drill. As a professional I had to admire it. There was absolutely no chance of the fly-posters getting away. All there was left for them to do was to give up their arms...

They chose to throw them: one long thick stream of glue left stripes on the police column, followed by a second and then a hail of brushes and brooms still full of the cold, sticky liquid.

One to one. It was worth fighting back against the police, especially as one cop was skating over the slippery ground as if he was going for an audition as a Keystone Cop! He was as good as any of them... He was shifting from foot to foot, his arms held out to help his balance, always on the verge of tumbling. Just as he was about to topple he reached for a colleague's shoulder, desperately hanging on to the gold epaulettes. The stitches gave way and as the white thread broke, the couple collapsed together.

The Bolshies took the opportunity to scatter, with the exception of a young boy with a wrinkled face who remained in the sticky hands of the forces of law and order. Three cops were holding on to him. Brutally, they took him up to the coach, clearly showing their desire to avenge themselves—and their force—for their humiliation.

The group had to go round the Packard to reach the police van. As he was going past the bonnet the young man threw me an anguished look, like a distress signal. I suddenly had the impression that, for him, I was the last man he would see before being plunged into the darkness.

There was no way to break the look other than by lowering my eyes. He was asking too much of me…

The back doors of the prison van closed with a great clanging and grating of iron. I took a while to get in gear, my fingers gripping the hand-brake, thinking about the hard times ahead for the fly-poster. Hours of suffering which, paradoxically, would bring him closer to the martyrs with whom he was expressing his solidarity.

The words slipped out before I understood where they came from.

'Poor fool… If you only knew…'

There wasn't a single poster in the Rue Thomas, but on the other hand it was impossible to park. Dozens of cars were parked up on the pavement including two official vehicles decorated with tricolour flags. Uniformed chauffeurs were hanging round the railings of the Fantin house and stamping their feet to keep warm. They blew on their hands, their heads pulled back between their shoulders, sending out thick clouds of steam.

I spotted a space, in a corner between a small wall and a plane tree. I was determined to get into it. The bumpers banged against the bark of the tree under the amused eye of the professionals. The soldier standing guard at the door asked me for my identity.

'René Griffon.'

He ran a finger of his thickly gloved hand down a list without coming across my name.

'Sorry, I'm under orders, I can't let anyone in except family and officials.'

'Tell Colonel Fantin that I'm at the gate. René Griffon. Here's my card.'

The guy grabbed the bit of cardboard and had it taken inside. The answer wasn't long in coming. In my favour. I went past the orderly and gave him a friendly tap on the shoulder as I went by.

It was even more difficult to find some space in the immense hallway on the ground floor. It seemed they'd passed the word around to present their regrets as soon as possible. Black was the dominant colour of the crowd. Only the multicoloured decorations pinned to the chests of the generals sitting on the couch broke the monotony of colour. I immediately felt ill at ease without being able to work out where this feeling of floating in cotton came from. Lack of sleep ... Suddenly going into an overheated room after the sharp cold outside ... Voices, conversations, feet scraping, the sound of china reached my ears in a sort of stew of sounds whose rhythm was slowed down and blurred.

An irresistible desire to yawn made me close my eyes. When I opened them again, Colonel Fantin was standing in front of me. He had disguised himself as a widower, from head to foot. However, his face denied the sadness of the rest of the outfit: his gaze was dry and more piercing than ever. Despite all his efforts he could not rid himself of a slight lift of the mouth which gave him an imperceptibly ironic or distant air, depending on whether you liked him or not.

He hissed through gritted teeth rather than speaking.

'How dare you come here today!'

His panicky reaction reassured me that I was on the right track.

'I've got to talk to you... The police called me, this morning...'

He turned on his heel after throwing out an order:

'Follow me!'

He plunged through the crowd without paying any particular attention to the people he bumped into. His rudeness brought out a flood of compassion: everyone thought, the Big Man is fleeing to conceal his pain. Fantin led me into a tiny room which I had not seen before. It led into a sort of workroom where gardening tools were kept. A spiral staircase for the servants led up to the first floor. Fantin locked the door then came up to me, his hands thrust into the pockets of his trousers.

'You should have warned me you were coming, we could have arranged a more discreet way to meet... The police are carrying out their enquiries.'

I had decided not to let anything pass as long as I had no idea what he was up to.

'It's all your own doing... The police would have had nothing to enquire about if you had told me about your rendezvous last night... You've used...'

The colonel cut me short in full flight.

'Come on, stop playing the outraged professional! When I

was advised to use your services, you were described to me as a scrupulously honest private detective … a sort of idealist caught between the need to earn your daily bread in a profession that is … shall we call it unique … and the desire to make others happy. That's what made me decide to take you on: I wanted to keep well away from the scum that infest your line of business!'

'That's Bob's version of the story. He likes a bit of melodrama.'

Fantin nodded his head in appreciation.

'So you traced it back to him … Congratulations! That just shows that your friend Bob underestimates you. Following his description, I felt sure that mentioning your old General Hordant would mean you would look no further … Sometimes we are the victims of our own illusions of grandeur …'

'No one escapes! While we're on the subject of Bob, you have to admit that you weren't very generous … A hundred francs to betray a friend … Judas's last dozen pieces must be worth a mint with inflation! Anyway, Bob is no different from anyone else, he opens his mouth when rich guys like you come along with your wallets wide open.'

Fantin jumped at the opening.

'You too … There are few people who are unmoved by the power of money. You didn't set up a deal like that just for the hell of it!'

He had caught me off guard and it took me a few seconds to reply with an air of great innocence:

'What deal?'

He breathed deeply and pronounced his words slowly to stop himself from shouting:

'Don't play the fool, Griffon... It would have taken only one word from me this morning for Inspector Aubry to arrest you under suspicion of murder. One word. So don't push it, my memory might come back...'

The colonel was at the end of his tether. All politeness, all reserve had dropped away. He'd lost all veneer of class. I was deliberately provoking him.

'What are you waiting for? Ring him. You've got nothing to tell him... Nothing, you hear me?'

'You're mistaken. I've got something that could take you to the scaffold... It took me a while to recognize you. A good idea, that big grey overcoat with the turned up collar that hid your face... I thought you had given up the job with the offer of an extra week's pay; your secretary seemed relieved... I pictured you celebrating... I was within inches of settling the affair and you ruined the whole thing. The sting was perfect.'

It was my turn to show surprise.

'What sting?'

'Come on, don't take me for an imbecile... You made me hang on for a week, without giving me any revealing information. In truth, you were putting all your energy into finding out who the blackmailer was. That's the reason why you attached so much importance to poor Emmanuel Alizan... He took you straight to the nurse from the sanatorium at Villepinte... I would never have suspected such a thing in a hundred years. Once you knew who it was, you made an agreement with him to suggest an exchange at Roissy-en-France. You knew that as soon as that happened I would get you out of the way... By intervening at the last minute, during the hand-over, you could double the stakes. And get the same amount of money out of me a second time... That's what happened, isn't it? But your elegant plot came unstuck... There were deaths...'

He had stretched his brains so much to put the pieces of the puzzle together that I didn't have the heart to contradict him.

'If you say so... How do you know I was there if I disguised myself so well?'

He had the smug smile of a poker player laying the ace of diamonds on the king.

'You should have hit harder, I've got a tough head. After being pistol-whipped I came to quite quickly... You were bent over my wife's body. The nurse's car had already left. You had taken your coat off... It wasn't hard to recognize you with that aviator's jacket and the cowboy trousers! I watched you, you got your car out from behind the shelter... A Packard with a damaged wing... You think there are a lot of them on the streets?'

'Why didn't you fire at me? You were armed.'

'How should I know if the papers were in your hands or the nurse's? A one in two chance... And the risk of missing you was too great; what happened next showed me I'd done the right thing... That's not the case for you: the share-out with your accomplice didn't turn out the way you wanted. It must be infuriating to leave such a sum behind...'

His reasoning appeared quite logical. But he didn't realize the most important thing: if I was at the rendezvous, it was because I had taken the liberty of opening his mail! He thought he had me at his mercy. I found it hard to find fault with the story he had just elaborated. I stayed silent for a long moment as I mentally checked off the night's events and compared them with Inspector Aubry's hypothesis. The attack had a stunning effect:

'You've forgotten one detail in all this...'

The colonel showed his condescension.

'Oh, yes, what's that?'

'First of all, thank you for your discretion but your statements to the investigative police carry other contradictions which don't spring from your desire to protect me.'

'What are you insinuating?'

'For example, you stated that the exchange of fire took place after your loss of consciousness since you didn't hear it. You know that's not true: the shots went off before you were laid out cold. I'm positive about that!'

Fantin leapt at this admission.

'So you admit it was you!'

'Perhaps, if you admit in turn to the difference in the order of events. Inspector Aubry will be very interested to share the secret... don't you think?'

'In any case, it forces us to attach even more value to our relationship... Just tell me how much you think your silence is worth. In the knowledge that I'll throw in my silence as part of the bargain. I'm rich and in a hurry...'

You could at least give him full marks for directness. I thought to myself that I had rarely walked in shit so deep. I had to go on at a steady pace not to sink in. I played for time.

'It's better not to be too hasty: the police are on the lookout. It would be neither to your advantage nor to mine to put them on the trail. When is your wife's funeral to take place?'

'In two days' time.'

'Very well. Let's agree on the day after the burial. I'll

telephone you your instructions... Until then, just keep quiet!'

His chest swelled at this insult: he had difficulty in swallowing my orders.

'What next... Do you realize to whom...'

I didn't give him time to finish and turned on my heel.

On the return trip I concentrated on driving fast, keeping my mind on the road. Once I got to Paris I left the car at the garage: I hadn't checked anything over the last three days: oil, water, battery, tyres, spark plugs...

The engine needed to be well-built to cope with such neglect! The boss was on the verge of tearing me off a strip, but he must have reminded himself that I was a customer. He held his tongue.

'Shall I take care of the paintwork at the same time?'

'No, I'll come by to pick her up tomorrow morning. I'm doing a lot of driving at the moment. By the way, don't forget to fill the tank and stick a twenty-litre can in the boot... You can't find a petrol-pump on every corner.'

He made a fuss, on principle.

'That's not very safe... Suppose somebody set you alight with a cigarette, your car would explode!'

I shrugged my shoulders and he beckoned to the apprentice to fill the can.

'I started cleaning it with Irène. If your guy has time on his hands...'

'OK. Do you need anything else?'

'Yes, do you know how many garages sell Cardens?'

He looked at me, dumbfounded.

'You want to put yourself on the list or... Don't tell me you're thinking of buying one of those heaps of junk! Not after a Packard!'

I reassured him.

'No, don't get upset. It's for work. I've got to make a list of all the cars of that make that are on the road in the area.'

'You can do that easily enough. It was shown a few weeks ago at the Salon de Paris. In October. The only argument the maker had to sell that rubbish was to say that it cost less than the radiator grille of the Hispano-Suiza H6 ... I would have preferred the petrol-cap: at least that's decorative! They must have unearthed about ten suckers ... No garage that took itself seriously would agree to keep a car like that in stock; they've got a reputation to keep up. I don't even know what I would do if one of those cars stopped here for petrol ... I think I would probably refuse!'

I interrupted his ruminations on questions of conscience.

'There must be an importer?'

He took me over to his office.

'Hang on; I've got the catalogue of the Paris exhibition somewhere in a corner ...'

He shuffled around piles of trade magazines, plans, boxes of spare parts, tools, before laying his hands on a large book with a stained cover where the two hundred and fifty firms were listed who took part in the first Salon after the war.

He opened it at the section on English cars and proudly showed me a picture of the Carden.

'That's the car you're looking for, isn't it?'

I immediately recognized the kind of toad on wheels which had carried off the stranger at Roissy-en-France.

'Her twin!'

At the bottom of the page, an outlined advertisement carried the name and address of the exclusive importer for France. I wrote it down in my notebook.

DURIAN. Dealer for CARDEN
19 Rue Danton
Levallois-Perret (Seine)

I said goodbye. Going home I took a detour by the Cité des Flamands. A Sicilian had just opened a grocer's and had all kinds of Italian products on offer. With his advice, I put together an instant meal: coppa, salami from the mountains, fresh pasta. Plus some wine from the Veneto. In short, it was my turn to get the dinner! Irène was waiting for me in the hallway, all rigged out. Velvet suit, little boots, hat. She put her coat on as soon as I put a foot in the door. I put the meal down on the table.

'Where are you going? It's almost four o'clock... Have you eaten?'

'Exactly, we've just got enough time.'

'Time for what? We had nothing fixed for today.'

She opened her bag and held out an invitation card to me.

'I got it before Christmas... I forgot about it but we just have to make an appearance. Even if only for quarter of an hour.'

The invitation was from one Liliane Courtais who was marrying a Raymond Laplace at four thirty at the church in Saint-Germain-de-Charonne.

'They can get married without us! Besides, it's the first time I've ever laid eyes on these names. Friends of yours?'

'Yes, Liliane is a childhood friend. I'd enjoy seeing her again disguised as a bride... We'll just go for a spin in the car and come straight back... OK?' I could never resist her mocking seduction, any more than the sweetness of her lowered tone; I interpreted these whisperings as promises. I was rarely mistaken.

'The car is at the garage. Being overhauled. I know the

area, the church is just in front of the Place Saint-Blaise station. With a bit of luck we'll be in time.'

We had to go all the way up the Rue de Flandre and Irène's high heels made a clacking sound to the rhythm of our forced pace. The train was in the station but the guard waited for us to get in the last coach before waving his red flag. The engine spat out a thick, black cloud of smoke that the wind blew down the train.

'It stinks as much as the metro!'

'You're never happy… At least the view is better.'

We had just crossed the Ourcq canal, following the Saint-Denis canal. I pointed out to her the cramped building of the abattoir, the metallic structures of the cattle stands. The scalloped roofs of the general stores that lined the road were reflected in the liquid surface of the channel, evoking images of Italy.

After a short stop at Belleville-Villette the train gradually picked up cruising speed again, helped by the downward slope of the route. Going past the double bridge where the Rue Manin and Rue Crimée crossed, the train dived under the Parc des Buttes-Chaumont and the hill at Belleville.

Welcome to the soot! A complete black-out right up to Charonne… Anyway, it was just as well. I liked the area of La Chapelle a hundred times more, despite its gasometers and regular traffic jams of lorries, than this area stuffed full of metalwork factories, and enamelling workshops… Going through it you quite often got a blast of acid up your nose when a worker, half-suffocated by working too long on top of the electrolysing dips, came out to get a breath of fresh air on the pavement.

One came across dozens of them like that, aged between

fifteen and forty at the outside... I avoided looking at the hands eaten away by chemicals, clenching my own hands in the depths of my pockets.

Irène dragged me away from my thoughts: we had arrived at the station. Now we only had to go a few hundred metres up the Rue Bagnolet.

There was a crowd gathered on the right of the Place Saint-Blaise, shouts, snatches of music reached our ears. Irène hurried forward.

'There's no point in running... The ceremony seems to be over; they're coming out...'

In reply she quickened her pace, beyond hope of my catching up, especially as the scene taking shape before my eyes gave me no desire to join in the celebration. Irène reacted in the same way and slowed down in her turn. She turned towards me, her face full of distress.

'No, it's not true! René, tell me it's not possible...'

I would have loved to have been able to contradict what she saw but my own repulsion could not have been written more clearly on my face.

The crowd of friends and relatives who had come to greet the newly-weds on the steps of the church stood a little to one side, on the square. On each side of the doorway there was a row of unfortunate men stuck in their wheel-chairs. A fine display of the different models available on the market. From the Vélocimane for those who had their lower limbs amputated to the Auto-Mouche by way of the Vélauto, a sort of motorized scooter. They had all polished up their motors: every spoke glimmered in the sun, their chests loaded with trinkets they lifted their heads high, jaws jutting.

The Guard of Honour of those who had donated limbs to the Cannibal Country... I leant over towards Irène.

'What are they doing here? Are they part of the Association of Broken Bodies?'

'Perhaps... I don't know... Anyway I hope they're not all relatives! It would be enough to make you put a gun to your head!'

Anyone who still could stood on tip-toe when the cloud of white lace emerged from the shadows. I could just make out the bride's smiling face hidden by a veil blowing around in the wind. The noise stopped suddenly when the ranks of mutilated men made an effort to produce their version of a guard of honour. Irène pinched me on the arm.

'Can you see the husband?'

'No, I don't get it... He should be coming out of the church...'

In front of us, a woman bent down to pick up a child in her arms. In a flash our gaze was fixed on the poor thing dressed in black which had braked at the top of the stairs.

Two men moved away from the crowd of guests. They went up to the husband and lifted him up to enable him to get over the obstacle. He couldn't have been much more than twenty, going by his smooth cheeks which Liliane stilled with the tips of her fingers in order to give him the prolonged kiss demanded by the photographers.

A cruising Renault taxi of the G7 Company was trying to get through the crowd in the hope of getting to the Rue Saint-Blaise. I signalled to him. Irène didn't move, hypnotized by the pitiful sight.

'Come on, let's go; it makes me feel ill.'

I pushed her into the back of the car.

'Head for Levallois-Perret. Rue Danton.'

The driver set the clock and got into first with a grinding of gears to make you scream.

'It complains but it gets there! The company trade mark! To be honest, this heap's done some mileage! I'm telling you, we were at the departure from Gagny in September '14 ... My longest trip: right up to the Marne! We were never paid but I'm not complaining; I'm not going to jump into a legal wrangle with the War Ministry for two or three cans of petrol ... A small sacrifice compared to those guys ... Especially as they're not all going to be so lucky as to fall on a kid as plucky as that young bride ... All the same it's very fine to come across a woman who has no hesitation in sacrificing herself for a wounded man ... He did it for his Motherland. I'm not over-sensitive normally, but things like that get you in the guts!'

He braked hard as he finished his sentence. As soon as the taxi stopped, he turned towards us, his eyes raised to the sky, took off his cap then brought his right hand, palm flat, up to his temple.

'Long live France'

Irène burst out laughing, a nervous laugh that signalled the onset of tears.

'We're in a taxi, not at the theatre ... Wait till you calm down and put your cap back on, with the peak aimed at Levallois-Perret!'

I didn't mean to hurt his feelings, but it would have taken too long to explain, to get him to see my point of view ... if he ever did! I couldn't help thinking to myself that if Jesus Christ himself came back to earth to convert mankind, even his gift of the gab wouldn't be enough to get round a taxi-driver's moral sense.

CHAPTER 10

Once we'd gone past the Porte de Champerret, we still had to cross the Levallois district, at least as far as the Seine. Rue Danton ran into the Quai Michelet, on a level with the tip of the island at the Grande Jatte. Everything reeked of work here: the tug-boats and their strings of barges weighed down in the grey water; the steam-driven cranes whose metal joints hiccuped under the strain of their loads, the countless clouds of smoke, ranging from wisps of white to dense black, which added continuously to the one huge cloud arching over the roof-tops. It was as if the buckets of sweat wrung out along the assembly lines of Clément-Bayard or Dion-Bouton could no longer be separated from the places and bodies where they had originated.

I settled up with the taxi-driver, without saying a word. The Durian Garage was on the corner of a blind alley, with an uneven pavement, stained by large patches of oil where sumps had been drained.

Irène walked with care, not putting any weight on her heels for fear of breaking them if she caught them between two paving-stones. The doors of the workshop were wide open. I went in first. A dozen workers were busying themselves around car chassis, bits of bodywork, engines on work-benches or hanging from pulleys. They all had on a kind of uniform: old clothes that no one bothered to mend any more and which everyone wore in three or four successive layers. If you were lucky the holes didn't match up ... They could be mistaken for tramps if it weren't for the grease stains on their hands, faces, hair ... and especially the interest which was kindled in their eyes when they caught sight of Irène's legs.

I couldn't think of a single tramp who had ever turned his head when a woman went by. Their whole desire was concentrated on drink whereas here the response was unanimous: they stopped working so they could appreciate them to the full.

A few moments of real life snatched unplanned out of the tedium of work! The boss hadn't heard us come in, but the racket coming to a sudden end, the hammering of sheet metal that gave way to the muffled roar of the street, had made him sense that something was up. He burst out of his office, a corner carved out at the end of the workshop.

He stopped abruptly and stuck his thumbs into the pockets of his work-jacket. He looked up at us. He was quite a heavy man, with dark red hair sticking out under a corduroy cap, his face divided by a dark, heavy moustache. He spoke in a high voice, which didn't seem to belong to him.

'What's your business?'

Before I could reply he turned towards the work-benches.

'You lot, are you working or what? It's not break-time, at least not by my watch ...'

The hammers which had been suspended for an instant beat down on the twisted metal with a bit more anger than before.

The big man with the falsetto voice didn't move. We had to give in and make our way right up to the sanctuary. Irène trod on my heels: she couldn't do anything but follow in my footsteps.

'Is this the Durian Garage?'

He pointed above the entrance with his right index finger.

'Yeah ... I think that's the name that's written on the sign.'

He put his thumb back in the pocket of his waistcoat and I caught sight of his left hand, which was deformed, swollen with scars which indicated multiple fractures underneath. He noticed me staring.

'Not very pretty, eh! Lucky I'm right-handed, otherwise I'd be finished as a precision engineer.'

'Was it the Germans who messed you up?'

He shook his head and the locks with the touch of red that slipped out from his cap whipped his face.

'No, not the Krauts ... A shitty Benz ... An apprentice switched it on while I still had my paws stuck in the engine. But the idiot wasn't in Jerry's pay ... I should know!'

Irène plucked my sleeve. She hauled herself up to ear-level while whispering loudly enough to be heard.

'Hey René, where is the car?'

The guy leapt to help her.

'You're looking for a car, Madam?... What model?'

I interrupted.

'We've heard people talking about the little English car, the Carden. It's highly spoken of.'

You would never have guessed by the face he pulled.

'Yes, but it depends on what you use it for ... I've got customers who've bought it and think they're driving a Levassor. If you don't drive around much, it's not worth going to the bother of getting a big limousine ... Do you do much mileage?'

'Yeah, quite a lot but I'm well equipped for it: with a Packard.'

The magic word for a car fanatic. Although Irène's legs had left him cold, the mere thought of the twelve cylinders of my luxury motor made him jump for joy.

'Is it outside? I don't get to see one of those every day.'

'No, it's being fixed. We came in a taxi ...'

A cold shower! It wasn't worth going into details and describing the dented wing: I didn't want to be taken for a savage. To underline the effect, I let drop a promise.

'I would have a reason to come back and see you if we did business.'

'I hope so ... If I understand rightly, the Carden is for Madam.'

As he spoke, he couldn't help but mimic those polite gestures that all tradesmen inflict on us, whether they be sellers of shoelaces or financial magnates, but his charade quickly took on a sinister air and his thumbs retreated at regular intervals into the depths of his waistcoat. Knowing that I drove a top of the range American car had put him completely at ease. If you thought about it carefully, pure chance had arranged things nicely: to come into the area in your best clothes, it couldn't have worked out better. We must have looked like a couple of suckers rolling in money. Long live the bride!

'Would you like to have a spin? I could explain all the details on the way.'

I agreed. The most difficult thing was to cram three people (of whom one was a redhead with broad shoulders) into the kind of bath-tub which was what the body of the car resembled. Irène opened the single side door and stepped over the seat to fit into the back. I was fine until the boss, having set off the motor with a single turn of the starting handle, got in front of the wheel. As a manufacturer's economy measure, the steering was neither on the right nor the left, but in the middle! Of course, we could have helped each other out by sharing the controls. The problem was that we would have had to react within split seconds when it came to the bends. In the same direction if possible.

'It's not big. In principle there are two seats: one in front, one behind... This is just to show you because it won't do the engine any good. I'm quite a weight! A three horsepower two-stroke... You get what you pay for...'

He went round the block of houses in low gear and we came back hugging the walls of the Bayard car factory.

'Have you seen inside that place?'

He spoke of it as if it were a museum.

'No... Are you allowed?'

'You bet! Country bumpkins come here after the Moulin Rouge and the Graff Restaurant! Their assembly lines are better than the ones at Ford... They move along on their own with a system of electric pumps. The most modern you can get. If it goes on like that you can get rid of the workers... There'll be nothing but machines!'

The Carden turned into the alleyway and came to a stop. I let out a sigh of relief; it was about time I stretched my legs. I had pins and needles up to my ankles and I couldn't feel the sole of my foot on the pavement, as if there were a layer of cotton wool between them.

The boss directed us over to the workshop.

'So, what do you think of it?'

Irène limited her response to a sugary smile while giving me a quick wink. The moment of truth was coming upon us but I felt very confident. The boss had definitely typed us as middle-class idiots unless he thought I was a playboy giving my tart a present! I plunged in without waiting a moment longer.

'I think we could do a deal quite soon. How long do you take to deliver?'

'You have to wait at least a month. As long as it takes to come from England.'

I tightened my lips to show my displeasure.

'Oh, that's a nuisance. You haven't got any in stock?'

'No, not at the moment. These modest little cars go very fast... I got the first ones in mid-December, after the Salon. About twenty of them. Ever since then, bang, cleaned out!'

'In such a short time... They certainly are successful. Are they Parisians like us who seem interested?'

A cloud had just burst above Levallois. The entrance was obscured by a curtain of rain. The boss turned his back to me suddenly to tick off one of his workers.

'Can't you see it's pouring! Take the two Citroëns in or all our work will be wasted!'

The mechanic obeyed sullenly. Before going out into the icy rain he covered his head and shoulders with an old potato sack which had been unstitched on one side. He went off, badly protected by his haphazard cloak.

'You have to keep your eye on them all the time. Not a moment's slacking... To come back to your question, most of the buyers have been people from the country who came to Paris for the Salon. They come once a year and they make sure they don't miss anything. Parisians take their time. They go and inspect the competition before they come knocking at the right door... They would be wrong not to indulge themselves. Don't you agree?'

I was on the right track and nothing in the world would have made me let go. It didn't cost me anything to agree with his opinions.

'Of course! I was just asking you out of interest: if we've got a month to spare before getting one of your cars, perhaps my wife and I could go and visit one of your clients. To get the owner's opinion... I don't know if that's something people do these days...'

Finally he decided to invite us into his office out of the wind and gusts of rain. A tiny paraffin stove balanced on a car radiator was enough to transform the room into an oven.

'Even if it's not the rule, we could make an exception for young people as friendly as yourselves.'

He had just pulled an impressive register out of a pile of documents and was leafing through it, snapping the pages between his fingers.

'There. I've told you nothing but the truth! Fifteen from the country, four from the Seine and surrounding area. Take your pick.'

I took all the time needed to copy out the four addresses written along the pale blue lines.

M. Joseph Gordon, 8 Rue Jean de la Fontaine, Neuilly-sur-Seine.
Mme Vve André Berthier, 17 Avenue de l'Opéra, Paris.
Mme Germaine Ghyka, Omnia, Boulevard Montmartre, Paris.
M. Daniel Sorinet, 65 Rue Bobillot, Paris.

I folded the piece of paper and slipped it carefully into a pocket of my wallet. It was time to take our leave without upsetting the apple cart. Sometimes it was enough just to linger a moment or two too long in a conversation like this to bring about catastrophe… However, Irène's presence by my side produced a string of miracles: the redhead was even kind enough to call a taxi for us.

'You could get pneumonia in weather like this. You might have to hang around for a hell of a long time: we're not on a main route; the G7 garage is on the other side of Levallois. You're lucky if you get two cruising around the area in a week!'

He hung up with a self-satisfied air.

'That's lucky, I happened to pick up an old friend, old man Picaud. He'll be here in two minutes…'

He had hardly got the words out of his mouth before the image of the bare-headed driver saluting France in his cab sprang to my mind. I could have wagered my car that they were two of a kind. Irène gave me a dig in the ribs with her elbow on the way out: we were obviously on the same wavelength.

The Renault escaped from the Marne had backed into the garage so we wouldn't get drenched but the driver must have regretted his manoeuvre as soon as he recognized us. I was sure that if it was just down to him, he would have left empty-handed, except that the old swindler had probably set his meter going as soon as he left the depot. Sure, he couldn't stand us, but that was no reason for him to lose a fare!

As I was throwing a last glance at the cars scattered around the garage my eye was caught by the Citroëns the mechanic had gone out to fetch in from the rain. Two old models done up like new. The guy was still getting it in the neck! Underneath the bodywork was beginning to wrinkle in sheets. A special trick in the area: rather than sanding off the rust, the local comedians didn't do any more than stick brown wrapping paper on the affected part. A couple of coats of paint and the customer in a hurry saw the green light ... At least until the weather decided to reveal all!

Once, before the war, one of my uncles braked too sharply and found himself with two halves of a car ... Luckily, on that particular day, he wasn't going too fast. When he was retelling the story he inevitably finished the anecdote by saying, 'It just goes to show it was a good second-hand bargain: I'm still here!' None the less, after that he always bought new ... Good old uncle!

The taxi had to go along the fortifications before it could enter Paris. On the side of the road were little cafés, each more sordid than the last, as if part of a pageant of misery. Le Philosophe, La Débine and so through the complete titles of Hugo, Zola or Eugène Sue ... An encyclopaedia of popular literature carved on rotten planks: L'Assommoir, Les Misérables, Aux Mystères de Paris ...

As the automobile industry developed, the area was gradually being swamped by businesses dealing in repair and renovation. Gangs of Moroccan labourers, tall skeletal characters, were taking over from the original workers from Brittany or the Auvergne among the smears of grease as well as the camp-beds.

Irène had had her eyes closed for some time. I felt her hair against my cheek as we went over a bump.

'Are you asleep?'

'No, I'm sick of the sight of all this ... I feel almost ashamed that we two have managed to struggle free. We've paid a price for it . . . They'll never have the slightest chance; the dice are weighted against them.'

She sighed, and without further ado, put her arms around my neck and pressed her face against mine. Her short rapid breaths tickled my lips. Without even kissing me she stuck out her tongue and, while swaying her head to some soothing internal rhythm, she began licking my lips with a caress of unimaginable softness. I lay back, tears in my eyes, overwhelmed with happiness. I only responded when she tried to enter my mouth with her moist tongue, and shot out my own. She fiercely refused to let me into her mouth, her forehead pressed against mine to the point of pain.

The driver, who was observing the scene in his rear-view mirror, didn't miss a second.

Irène gave in near the Porte de Flandre. We were going through the gate when her lips parted. The struggle finished with a kiss that took us straight to heaven.

The patriot from G7 had a sense of what was needed:

'Rue de Maroc. You've arrived.'

When all's said and done, it was just in time; two more minutes on the road and the cab rescued from the Marne would have been turned into a red light district!

Irène was in an affectionate mood; after making love she used all her powers of seduction to keep me at home but Fantin's ultimatum kept me from following my natural inclinations. Having run out of arguments, as I got to the door, my jacket over my shoulder, she tried the taxi trick again with a similar result.

Half an hour later I managed to escape to freedom without

too much resistance: she knew from experience it wouldn't have worked a third time.

I felt up to checking out two of the four addresses that evening. I cast my choice on the customers of the Durian Garage who lived in the heart of Paris, near the Rue du Maroc.

Widow Berthier, Avenue de l'Opéra, and Germaine at the Omnia on the Boulevard Montmartre. It seemed unfortunate that it should be the two women. I would have preferred to tackle the two men in the first instance, that seemed to fit better with what I had seen in Roissy. I consoled myself by thinking that the widow probably had a lover somewhere in her possession and set off towards the Opera House.

The apartment block was at the other end of the avenue on a level with the Pyramides metro, with an imposing façade in carved stone, opening on to a hall large enough to contain three apartments the size of mine. I had barely reached up to the bell when a doorman in uniform appeared.

'Yes, sir, are you looking for somebody?'

Talk about being discreet, I could have taken some lessons from him.

'Mme André Berthier, on behalf of M. Durian …'

He looked me over from head to toe with the neutral glance of a professional, giving nothing away.

'I'm sorry, sir, she won't be back before eleven o'clock.'

I went up the Boulevard Montmartre to the Omnia, a cinema I sometimes went to, if there was anything interesting. There was nothing interesting that day: the posters announced *Popaul and Virginie, The Sacred Tiger* and *The Christmas Stocking*. About a dozen people were standing around in the shelter of the metal columns. From far away the entrance looked like an entrance to the metro, one by Guimard, if it hadn't been for the cast-iron peacocks that framed the name of the cinema. As I approached the would-be spectators huddled together to close ranks: any stranger who went over the no man's land marked out by a line of tiles that ran along the pavement was seen as a queue-jumper. Even the war-wounded no longer dared march up to the front with their crutches held high. There were bronze statues in their honour in every square in France, that was plenty.

A big man in a checked suit barred my way and looked me up and down; the fat man knew what I was going to say. He heaved over to the side, leaving the way open to the box-office.

I leant over so that my face was on a level with the window pierced with many holes. The cashier interrupted her knitting.

'Can you tell me where I can find Mme Ghyka?'

'Yes, of course, that's me.'

I was speechless for a few seconds, the time it took me to pull myself together. Unconsciously, I had outlined to myself an image of the typical driver of a Carden: a sedate middle-aged lady, or probably even older, beginning to put on weight and loaded with enough money to be able to treat herself to a life-sized motorized toy. In fact I was confronted by a twenty-year-old doll, pregnant up to the eyeballs, who was knitting baby vests, mixed pink and blue, while waiting to deliver the goods.

'I thought you would be different....'

My voice trailed away. She smiled.

'Are you disappointed?'

'No, quite the reverse... I'm not going to flirt with you in your state... You see, I wanted to buy a Carden and I was told that you had one...'

'Yes, that's right. You're well-informed, I've had it for a month. Can I ask how you...'

I replied before she had time to finish.

'The Durian Garage at Levallois. They haven't got any more in stock for a demonstration. They gave me your address... If I could see it...'

'That's not difficult, I've put it in the Borker Garage, it's on the corner of the Passage des Panoramas. Give my name to the caretaker, he'll let you in.'

The carriagework of the tiny English car was as shiny as the one in Roissy-en-France. Just one detail, it was as light as the other one was dark. I bent over and inspected the edge of the metalwork without much expectation of finding any traces of a recent paint job. The original ivory... I put a line through 'Mme Germaine Ghyka, Omnia, Boulevard Montmartre, Paris' under the intense and suspicious gaze of the guardian of the establishment.

CHAPTER 11

I still had a bit less than an hour to kill before the widow from the Opéra was due to return. I hadn't had a bite to eat since lunch and hunger was gnawing at my insides. The fragrances from a brasserie kept me going as far as the garage. Just breathing in the smells from a kitchen as you went by was enough to delay the famine. Unfortunately it's not the kind of experience that has a lasting effect: ten minutes later my body was calling for attention once again.

I leant against the bar of a brasserie and ordered a beer and sausages.

'Strasbourg or Frankfurt?'

Business definitely had fewer principles or a shorter memory than Irène. I responded to the provocation.

'Frankfurters.'

The waiter confirmed the order:

'You're on!'

I took up a lookout post at a quarter to eleven on the corner of the Rue Sainte-Anne, leaning up against the window of a ladies' hairdresser. The area seemed very lively, full of single men who eyed me strangely as they slowed down to pass me by. At first I thought they were responding to the advertisement behind my back: 'Rediscover your youth here. FLOREINE

Beauty Cream.' I changed my place and chose the blank metal blind of a tailor 'Men, Women and Children' but the single men continued to prowl. At least they made the time go faster: the widow Berthier was slightly later than forecast by the doorman but I didn't regret my extra twenty minutes' lookout. The Carden that stopped in front of the entrance was fitted with solid wheels while the one I was looking for was an ordinary model with spoked ones. I pulled the sheet of paper out of my pocket to cross out another line: 'Mme Vve Berthier, 17 Avenue de l'Opéra, Paris.' Not much use but it was part of the ritual of an investigation; I still felt on the ball enough to keep hold of four addresses and operate by elimination!

I didn't take in the meaning of the continuous circling of ageing beaux until it came to going back up the Rue Sainte-Anne ... Three or four times I was lured by discreet whistles from the shadows of recessed doorways. You didn't have to be clairvoyant to work out who they came from: until a short while ago they didn't go beyond the gardens of the Champs-Elysées ... It was evidently time that I brushed up on my night geography.

In front of me an older man let himself be accosted by a young kid of fifteen or sixteen. Following a signal the old guy disappeared into the entrance of the block of flats.

I began to laugh out loud, standing stock still on the pavement, thinking of those idiots who had taken me for a rent-boy a little while ago. I went back up towards Opéra. When I arrived at the square, I hurried towards the metro. With a bit of luck when I changed at République I could catch the last train on line five which would take me to Place d'Italie. Even the special police didn't venture out in the area around

Butte-aux-Cailles once night had fallen without making sure their arses were covered... There were a lot of stories going around about this area. The rag-and-bone men, the Bièvre, the stench of decay... and yet you were more likely to come across old tramps pissed as newts than young hoods. The adventurous were more likely to get mugged than seduced. Or you had to be prepared for a bumpy ride if you went with a woman from the housing estates.

It took your breath away; the rag-and-bone men and their families were crammed in, in their hundreds, in block after block as repulsive as the contents of their wheelbarrows. You didn't have to see the buildings to understand the danger: the heavy stench that emanated from the blocks of houses was quite enough to put the tourists off!

As a matter of caution I avoided going too near the danger zone. Number 65 Rue Bobillot was on the corner of the Rue du Moulinet, two steps away from the Station Balnéaire de la Ville de Paris, a complex comprising baths-showers-swimming-pool. The building was out of keeping: red brick in an area of dull colours. A wooden framework around the windows underlined the incongruous, misplaced character of the architecture.

The address unearthed at Levallois turned out to be a shabby hotel. You only had to look at the windows to know what it was like. More than half the openings had no curtains, several panes were striped with bands of sticky tape, as in the days of civil defence when Big Bertha was firing.

Paris was overflowing with these lodgings let by the day, occasionally by the week, which gave shelter to the masses of people from the country who came to seek their fortune in the capital.

Despite frequent raids by the police the owners rarely bothered to fill in the forms or the registers. By law the client was supposed to write his name in … So if he didn't know how to read … They were businessmen, not public scribes!

Hôtel des Fondeurs. A very obvious name given that part of the Rue du Moulinet was taken up by the dusty buildings of a foundry. The workers must have provided most of the clientele.

I climbed the three steps leading to the hotel from the street and followed a damp corridor lit by a dim bulb. The entrance hall, which was the size of a cupboard, was in a corner on the right behind a glass door. A counter had been fitted in under the stairs leading up to the bedrooms and a series of keys were hung up on hooks under the stairs. A large red-faced man, who was leaning up against the wall with his eyes half-closed, jumped when I pushed open the door. He rubbed his eyes to wake himself up. Unless it was that he couldn't get over the surprise: a client on the stroke of midnight, it couldn't happen that often in view of the atmosphere outside!

I propped my elbow on the counter, taking care to avoid the over-filled ashtray and some half-empty bottles of Belgian beer.

'Good evening, how are things?'

The ruddy-faced man was quite lively, even if he was just coming out of the fog.

'I don't suppose you've come here just to enquire after my health …'

I tightened my lips. The trace of a smile.

'Nor to tuck you up. There's not even a dog outside and all the cafés are shut … I thought that us two could have a little chat. A night with nothing to do drags on …'

He plonked his elbow down next to mine before resting the bundle of double chins which hung down from his cheeks on his thumb and index finger which disappeared into the flesh.

'You're new here . . . I'm paid up with the police, check it out . . . If you've come to rake up a bit extra, you've come knocking at the wrong door. If you're looking for a drink, you'd better move it, the bar across the road closes in five minutes!'

Already he was less amusing than at the beginning of his act. I forced myself to stick with the banter.

'I was going to have a drink and I was expecting to offer you one. A way of passing time . . . I'm not on the street . . .'

As I spoke I undid my jacket to bring out my wallet. I snapped a 5-franc note between my fingers. The guy did everything but touch his forelock.

'I like the way you get the old chat going . . .'

I stuck the note under an empty bottle.

'Firstly, I'm a private eye. Not a cop. I work on my own account. Secondly, I'm looking for a guy called Daniel Sorinet. He gave this up-market joint as his address recently. The note's yours if you'll cast an eye over your records.'

He stifled a yawn with the back of his hand.

'The files can tell you more lies than a dentist . . . I've got everything sorted out up here . . .'

He rapped his head with the knuckles of his fist.

'A real store-cupboard! Sorinet you said . . . The name rings no bells. Is it an old story?'

'A month at the very most.'

He pulled the note towards him and slipped it into his pocket, first having folded it carefully.

'Sorry, I can only tell you how it is. No Sorinet on the register … Is there a woman involved?'

I didn't want either to pull the wool over his eyes or to inform him.

'Yes, a divorce. The usual thing.'

There was nothing left for me except to follow up the trail of Gordon, Rue Jean de la Fontaine in Neuilly. I had no illusions, if Sorinet had given a false address, one might as well be looking for a friend's tibia in the ossuary at Douaumont! I hesitated in the shrunken space which passed as a hallway before I could pluck up the courage to leave. Too cold. The last metro must have been put away a while ago. At that time of night there was fierce competition for the few taxis that ventured forth into the area. I had one of those furtive moments when you look with envy on the job of night porter. Red-face brought me back to reality.

'Anyway, what kind of a mug has he got, your Sorinet?'

The hotelier wasn't averse to a bit of company. Now he was trying to spin out the discussion.

'They've only given me a very vague description … I know he often goes out in a big dark coat … A burly guy, probably young … That's all I've got to work on …'

'And his woman, is that all she knows about him! Are you pulling a fast one?'

It's always a mistake to look down on people you're talking to; despite his appearance as a slob, his brain was all there. I changed tack.

'OK, so it's not a question of a divorce but that doesn't change anything, I'm paying the rent by following him …'

He fumbled under the counter to haul out two bottles of beer.

'I wish you the best of luck to get your paws on him! You got nothing else by way of information?'

'On him, no. Except that he drives around in a little English car, a Carden.'

The porter stared at me, his interest suddenly caught by my reply. He poked his big ruddy face between the beers.

'That's not the kind of little toad on wheels that has the motor at the front and a fan belt to work the wheels at the back?'

My hopes were raised. I muttered.

'Yes, why?'

'Well, one of our clients used to get around in a machine like that. Only he wasn't called Sorinet… Shady characters, I've known hundreds round here, but him, well, if you'll pardon my saying so, he beat all the records! His name was Goyon… Armand Goyon. Room 14.'

He struck himself again, this time on the forehead with his index finger.

'It's all up here… There's more in there than in *Illustration*! Once it's there, it's there for ever…'

'Is he still at the hotel?'

'No, not for the time being. He's moved out.'

I felt I was on the right track. The Carden, the false names, moving out in a hurry after the events at Roissy, everything was falling into place perfectly. Too well perhaps…

'Has he left a forwarding address for the mail?'

He paused to give his reply more effect.

'Better than that. He hasn't finished removing all his junk.

Books, papers ... He's paid for the room until tomorrow midday. He should have come by but his room's been empty for two days now. If there's no news tomorrow, I'll put all his shit in the boiler. Unless he comes back between now and then like he said he would ...'

'I think I'll stay around and try my luck.'

He managed to slip me into the room next to number 14 at the special detective rate: on a par with the Côte d'Azur. With one small difference: the window didn't open out on to the sea!

On the other hand he was going to wake me up if Sorinet-Goyon showed up and would call a taxi at once to tail him. I fell asleep as soon as I lay down; the pace that Irène had set me was beginning to tell. The art of sleuthing demanded the fitness of an Olympic professional while I was only an amateur on the downward curve at the end of the season.

A while later I thought I could hear a creaking through my sleep. I sat up in bed, and pricked up my ears. The night porter came up on tip-toe.

'It's seven o'clock, I've finished my shift. He hasn't turned up but you never know: he's got until midday. You can't mistake him, you'll see he's a big bloke, young, twenty-five at the most; got a face like a boxer. He's had his hair shaved, at least what's left of it. OK? I'm going to turn in now, the sheets are calling and they're well-earned ...'

He shook my hand and disappeared. I sat without moving for a few minutes, yawning and stretching. I had slept without waking once, a dreamless sleep, with no memories, hours wiped out of my life. I opened the window thinking that the fresh air would bring me back to life. The wall of the building opposite, only fifteen metres away, was covered with a bovine ad on a faded blue background. Publicity for Laughing Cow Cheese.

It must have been about ten years old, dating from well before the dairy king was picked up at the frontier, his motor loaded with gold destined for Kaiser Wilhelm!

Charlie Chaplin couldn't have done it better: the next day hundreds of Parisians gathered on the Rue Blaise Desgoffes, in the sixth district, for the most important battle of the yoghurts of all time... Fresh cream, butter, packs of milk, tubes of concentrate, the whole range went. Buses skidded in 30 per cent fat content and passers-by found on their soles a mixture of Gervais and dust which could be traced right into the heart of the Latin Quarter.

That time I'd shouted as loudly as the rest, as loudly as my mate Gonnet.

At that time, it was less dangerous to attack a cheese shop in the heart of Paris than to paddle in the waters of the Rhine. The cow must have been killing herself with laughter thinking about it.

I left the hotel to take up my post at the bar of the Café des Nageurs on the corner of the Rue Bernard, opposite the bathhouse. From here I could see down the Rue du Moulinet as well as the entrance to the hotel. The Carden came into sight just before ten as I was downing my third coffee. The guy had left his lights on even though it was full daylight by now. I couldn't make him out, his face was hidden by the edge of the hood. I could only see his hands, his grey overcoat and the bottom part of his face. The bodywork of the car was splattered with mud and earth; clearly the driver was not as painstaking as I was. He was driving fast but to my relief he stopped abruptly in front of the furnished rooms and got out.

The night porter at the hotel was a good judge of build, Sorinet-Goyon reached at least one metre ninety and his large shoulders stretched the cloth of the coat. He glanced round the surrounding streets then went down the corridor. I fixed his features in my memory, one by one: square face, thick eyebrows, prominent cheek-bones, open brow, hair closely cropped. As to the clothes there was not much to say. Apart from the heavy coat I could just make out the cuffs of a pair of trousers of grey material and a pair of large walking boots.

I called a taxi on the phone and a G7 drew up in front of the pavement two minutes later. The bloke hadn't shown himself in the meantime.

'Where are we going, boss?'

'For the time being, we stay put... Then follow the Carden. You'll stay on her trail, she'll show us where the end of the line is. Have you got plenty of petrol?'

The driver winked at me in the rear-view mirror.

'Don't worry about that; I'm not going to be shaken off by a shoe-box on wheels... Are you part of the men in uniform?'

I put my finger to my lips.

'Sh... It's your turn now!'

The guy who called himself Sorinet at the garage and Goyon when he was renting a room had just reappeared, his arms full of boxes. He put them in the back of his car and sat behind the wheel again. He went straight to the west of Paris, Odéon, Concorde, Etoile. The whole length of the journey I was convinced that he was heading for the garage in Levallois without having much of an idea of what linked Sorinet to the redhead. I dropped the idea when the Carden plunged into the network of roads in Neuilly, between the Seine and the first trees of the Bois de Boulogne. The car stopped in front of a huge well-to-do house on three floors, fronted by a large garden.

'Shall I park behind?'

'No, certainly not... Go by as if it's nothing to do with you and turn into the little road on the right.'

The taxi overtook the Carden. I looked through the rear window; the driver had already got out and was busy getting the boxes out of the body of the car. Two other people came out to meet him to give him a hand. Clearly he was going to move in... From the slums to the posh area with nothing in between! I made a note of the address, 77 Rue Breteville, Neuilly-sur-Seine, before getting a ride home.

Irène was waiting for me with bad news: Aubry was insisting that I go and see him immediately at police headquarters. He wouldn't say any more on the phone. I had a vague idea of the kind of information he was hoping to get out of me...

In return, as I was busying myself buttering some bread, I told Irène how I had spent the time up to my excursion to Neuilly. She came closer, intrigued.

'Why are you laughing to yourself like that?'

'Was I laughing?'

'Yes, sure you were... You seem in a good mood. Are you going to tell me why?'

I put down the knife and the piece of bread.

'I don't know... It must be the laughing cow's head, on the box...'

Her glance went backwards and forwards between the box and my face.

'You're never quite frank when you spend a night out! You'd be better off thinking about Aubry and his expression than that of a cow.'

She was right. Unfortunately, seen from that point of view, it was a lot less funny!

CHAPTER 12

The day didn't promise to be a rest cure; there was plenty to do. I went straight to the garage. A damp mist curled around the riverbanks and warehouses. You could barely make out the waters of the Ourcq. I wouldn't have been surprised to hear the sailors hailing from barge to barge with a foghorn.

The Packard reigned over the centre of the workshop, spruced up for the passing out. The wing was back to its original shape, just a touch brighter than the rest of the bodywork.

'Are you pleased? She's as good as new; we've tarred it underneath. To make sure it doesn't rust. You don't have to worry what you do, with metal as thick as that. You won't get any holes for the next ten years!'

I went up close and ran my hands over the paintwork.

'Fantastic. Ask your apprentice to take her out, while I settle up with you... I'm in a real hurry.'

He climbed on to the running board and leant over the dashboard to work the levers. The motor purred at the first turn of the starter. He backed off with a look of self-satisfaction.

'Like clockwork!'

Then he called his assistant over.

'Hey, kid... Take the car outside, and handle her as gently as your sweetie...'

The boy came over, blushing. He hauled himself on to the front seat while we went to the office. I laid out fifteen 10-franc notes on the counter while the grinding of an abused gearbox made me grit my teeth.

The boss simply exhaled from his nose while deflating like a punctured tyre. He swallowed his anger and put the notes away in a drawer.

'I've put two jerry-cans of petrol in the boot, in case you're going a long way. You can relax, she'll take you to the ends of the earth.'

Before driving off, I slipped a 50-centime piece to the apprentice.

'No hard feelings …'

The experiment they'd been trying out at the Rue Caumartin didn't seem to have spread to any other areas over the last few days: all the roads I took to the police headquarters were two-way.

Inspector Aubry amused himself by making me wait in the corridor under the phlegmatic gaze of a cop very near retirement. To look at him you couldn't help but think that the first chase would do for him. Just covering the hundred paces between office 28 and the toilet made him wheeze.

Aubry made his presence known after showing his preceding visitor out. He gestured me to come in.

'So this enquiry on Colonel Fantin's behalf, how's it going? Have a seat.'

The strategy was a bit crude. I was expecting something better from him.

'No problem … I made the point when we saw each other the other day: Fantin terminated our contract before his wife died. I stopped everything straight away. I'm not mad enough yet to work on credit...'

He did no more than smile.

'You're right, Griffon, I forget things now and again. It's not surprising with all this work they pile on us! Anyway I'm not going to complain about it... After our meeting I drew up a statement based on what you had said...'

He took a typed sheet of paper out of a folder.

'... If you could just have a look over it and sign underneath. Unless there's some detail or phrase that you want to change.'

I grabbed the piece of paper. I took as long as I needed to read it carefully, down to thinking about where the commas went. The text summed up, in classic bureaucratic language, the story I had concocted for him the day after the events at Roissy-en-France. I came across Irène's name.

'It's pretty accurate in general... I hope there's no catch! You didn't have to name my girlfriend. She's nothing to do with this; she makes the appointments.'

'You have a knack of reversing the roles, Griffon. I didn't invent her... You told me about her. She's the only person able to support your alibi for that evening. Take her name out of the statement and I would have to think of you...'

He paused intentionally to add weight to his conclusion.

'... in a less friendly way.'

I signed without any further discussion.

'Is that all?'

He stood up, his face beaming, making no effort to hide his satisfaction. I turned away from him and reached for the door handle. This was the moment he chose to reveal his trump card.

'Yes, that's all for this morning... While you're here, go by the laboratory with your car. It's an American model, a Double-Six, isn't it?'

I nodded, my eyes glued to the woodwork. He went on.

'One of our teams has managed to pick up the tyre tracks of the car that was parked behind the bus shelter, at Roissy. They're not all that clear but they might do the trick. You're not the only one on the list, we're checking out dozens ... Is that O.K?'

'Yes, sure. I'll try to call by during the day, just for the record ... I know what the answer will be!'

Aubry tapped me on the shoulder three times.

'So do I ... The question is whether it's the same answer ...'

I left the headquarters and walked to the Packard which was parked round by Notre-Dame. I had to get four new tyres as quickly as possible, preferably used ones, and burn the ones that had been in Roissy. Bob was the only one who could help me out in record time, the problem was that he would use it to clear himself with Aubry at the same time. The rules of the game for him, you buy something in order to sell it!

In short there was nothing left but to hope for a miracle and the powers of invention of the Rue de Flandre garage!

Half-way there the connection 'Headquarters-Carden' popped up in my mind. I turned back on my tracks, which brought me a suspicious glance from the guard.

Robert, a friend from before the war, which means a guy I used to hang around with at the working girls' dances in 1912 and 1913, spent his time broadening his arse in the offices of the headquarters. I contacted him from time to time and he never looked down his nose at my money ... If every record that he dug out over the years had been paid for at the same rate, he'd have been richer than Rockefeller.

This time my entry into the main office clearly didn't have the usual effect on him. He blended into the background, the same dirty wood colour as his desktop, the same oily appearance. Even down to the lines on his face which looked like the dirty crease on the covers of the files. His colleagues, twenty or so busy bureaucrats, looked more or less like carbon copies of the original who was in front of me.

Not quite: Robert didn't dare look me in the eye. He stayed bent over his spotted blotter, a quartermaster sergeant about to fuss over a line in the inventory.

He whistled through his yellowing teeth rather than spoke.

'What are you doing here... You're mad!'

'I need a favour from you. It won't take long.'

He put his pen back in the ink-well.

'Go to the john...'

I was about to lay into him when he finished what he was saying:

'... I'll join you in five minutes.'

He couldn't have suggested a worse place to meet. I was driven to wishing I had a gas mask once again. Robert let me stew for a long quarter of an hour in this stench which soaked into the marrow of your bones. Finally he showed up. I was full of admiration: he breathed easily, his nostrils wide open. The stink didn't seem to upset him unduly.

He fumbled nervously through his pockets and found relief in some lumps of sugar.

'Do you want one?'

Two grey cubes taken from the counter of some bar were poised in the palm of his hand.

'No thank you.'

I would have felt as if I were eating cubes dipped in brandy smelling of shit instead of cognac!

He swallowed them.

'I crunch on a couple in the middle of the morning. I suffer from hypoglycemia ... The shakes in other words ... It started as soon as I saw you ... There's a lot of talk about you here, because of the death of the colonel's wife ... I don't want to get into any trouble.'

He was trying to sort out where he stood, to assess the value of the risk.

'I know. I'm not going to stick around here for long. The whole business should be cleared up in a few days ... That is if you can give me a hand. I'll make it worth your while.'

He coughed to clear his throat.

'You'd have to up the stakes a fair bit. It's getting difficult to help you, even if you are an old friend ...'

'I'm sure it is. I need to know the name of a guy who goes around calling himself Sorinet and Goyon. I know what he looks like, a beefy young character with a square face, half-bald ...'

'I don't need a description of him, the names are enough. I'll come back with everything I can find.'

I was about to pass out. By standing on the toilet rim I was able to reach the fanlight and open it with the tips of my fingers. The blast of air instantly revived me. I got out two 10-franc notes and gave them to Robert as soon as he came back again. The notes joined the fragments of sugar in the depths of his pockets.

'I had a bit of difficulty finding your two names. I nearly went straight past them: they had been crossed out of the central file . . . Sorinet and Goyon were both killed during the war. They were under surveillance before that; they were fellow travellers in the anarchist movement. Politicos. They joined in the movement to reappropriate flats. Those incidents involving Cochon . . . Do you remember? He led us a merry dance.'

'Yes, I vaguely remember . . . What use is it to him to go around assuming the identity of dead men?'

'You can't imagine what a mess the war made of the civil service files. The archives of towns occupied by the Germans were lost or destroyed . . . Everyone's thrashing around, they've got as much work as in an arms factory! The anarchists are no fools, they hand the identity cards of their mates killed during the war around among themselves. Often it's the families that give them to them. If they're arrested the local inspector does a routine identification without double-checking the name. And for a good reason! They're only here in the back-files.'

Robert stopped and made to go back to his desk. I stopped him.

'Wait, these two anarchists were part of a group of squatters of empty flats, is that right?'

'Yes, that's what I've just told you. Why?'

'I won't bother you again for a good while but it's essential that you get me the photographic files from before the war on the Sorinet-Goyon team . . . There can't be hundreds of them. I might well find the guy I'm looking for in that lot.'

He rustled the notes hidden in his pockets. The characteristic sound of a call for money reached my ears.

'You're asking for the impossible . . .'

It was only a way of raising the price. If I went on spending the money from Fantin at this rate, I would have to hurry up and wrap up the investigation before I found myself out of pocket.

'It's a deal, I'll double the rate.'

I paid him up front and he left for a short while. The impossible would be done in minutes!

I took the opportunity to relieve my bladder in the urinal. I chose my moment badly: a short-legged old lady pushed open the door, her arms loaded with dirty towels. She put the soiled linen down on the wash-hand basin and stood next to me, without saying a word. She stood on tip-toe while I cupped my hand as a shield to hide my sex from her gaze. I slid a furtive, curious look in her direction but she didn't seem to pay any attention at all.

I rehoused my organ without taking the time to shake off the drips, only to realize that she had simply come to unhook the used towel which was now heaped up with the rest of the load. She left, thanking Robert with a nod of the head as he held the door open for her. As soon as she was out of sight down the end of the corridor he held out a pile of cards about fifteen by twenty centimetres in size. The top half of each one had on the back the three official identity photos: profile, full face, profile, then the official description of the person. On the front were the reasons for a file being opened and the summary of the police record.

Sorinet and Goyon were first in the pile, followed by a show-case of militant anarchism: men with bald heads, with beards, with glasses, with the expression of hallucinating poets, hair sweeping their shoulders, civil servants in evening dress with bow ties and top hats... the owner of the Carden was hiding at the bottom of the pile between a young woman who specialized in revolutionary abortions and a forger.

My Sorinet-Goyon was in fact called Francis Ménard, born at Ivry-sur-Seine, a librarian by profession. He wasn't wanted for much before '17: a few illegal occupations of private property, taking part in a few demonstrations that ended badly... Now they were looking for him for 'desertion in the face of the enemy in May '17'.

Nowadays the penalty wouldn't be much more than three to five years in prison near Toulon; before the armistice, he would have faced the firing squad.

He could count himself lucky, he'd managed to save his skin. Those who were no longer here to say the same thing could be counted in platoons.

Walking back to the car, I decided to follow the trail leading to the appropriation of apartments. Francis Ménard and the friends whose identity he had taken over were at the time part of the 'Tenants' Trade Union', an anarchist group that had had its moments of glory in the two years preceding the war.

The whole of Paris used to follow the exploits of their spokesman, Georges Cochon, and his confrontations, which always included a large dose of humour, for the rehousing of working-class families.

Paris high society followed as well, although its laughter was nervous.

I remembered certain episodes such as the day of action 'Against the Tyranny of the Concierges' during which the Cochonnards' commandos put fleas, bugs and cockroaches through the keyholes of the concierges' doors! One day, I had also come across a procession of the 'badly housed' who were going up to take over the barracks at Château d'Eau from the soldiers. They were marching in serried ranks behind their band, 'The Cacophony of Saint Copy-Cat', a heterogeneous group with music scored for saucepans, ladles, billy-cans, tins...

The Socialist Party flags fluttered in the middle of the procession, mixed in with the black standards, and it wasn't unusual to come across the happy face of a Member of Parliament from that party. The party paper gave inflammatory accounts of the events and blamed everything on their *bête noire*, the Prefect Lépine.

Perhaps the reporter from that time was still at the rag despite all its ups and downs. I tried my luck.

It felt as if a Soviet revolution was in full swing at the office of the newspaper in the Rue Montmartre.

I gathered that an important conference was coming up in Strasbourg and that the corridors of *L'Humanité* seemed to be the ideal place to make or break alliances. I recognized Marcel Cachin by his impressive moustache, standing alone, his back to the wall.

The representatives-to-be milled around him but he remained unmoved by their agitation. I slipped past groups of people talking, catching here a name, there a word. 'Lenin', 'the conditions', 'reconstruction'... Finally I managed to reach Jules Guesde's old comrade.

'I believe you're Marcel Cachin?'

He was looking through me and my question made him jump. He stared at me.

'Yes, indeed. Did you want to see me?'

I, in turn, could not repress a thrill at the sound of his voice. Even his worst enemies could not hide their admiration for his gifts of oratory, his lyricism, the absolute hold that he had over crowds.

A worthy successor to Jaurès, for the editorship of the newspaper as well as in Parliament.

I took hold of myself.

'No, not exactly... I'm looking for the journalist who was covering the activities of the "Tenants' Trade Union"...'

He smiled and the movement of his lips had the effect of putting his moustache on a level with his nostrils.

'Oh, Cochon's troop! What a team... They gave us as much fun as any serial in the papers... It brought a note of humour to the editorial meetings. The events of the day didn't give us much cause to celebrate. As far as the journalist concerned, I think it was Lecointre if my memory serves me right. I'm not quite sure. Wait a minute...'

He went up to a frail-looking man of about forty who was trying to convince his audience of the correctness of his analysis. He interrupted him for a few moments before coming back to me.

'It's as I thought, Lecointre was responsible for following the movements of Cochon and his friends. Sadly, the comrade is no longer with us, he was killed in the war like so many others. We were not spared... But is it Lecointre or his articles that interest you?'

'His articles in principle but I would have liked to have heard him give an account of what he saw. It's difficult to get everything into an article, it can't help but be incomplete... Can one have a look at them?'

Cachin showed me a door at the end of the corridor.

'All the back numbers are in there, dating from 1904. Ask

Francine to help you, she knows practically every article off by heart; she'll make the work easier for you.'

He moved off with his calm gait, and, after taking stock of the different groups, threw his lot in with four old socialists who looked like senators and who were huddled in discussion.

I knocked loud enough to be heard above the noise. A female voice with a hoarse rasp told me to come in.

Cachin's 'Francine' was an enormous woman, pathologically obese, her blonde hair pulled back in a ponytail, as if she was trying to draw attention to her puffy features. She seemed to be trapped behind her desk and the piles of newspapers and books which cluttered the space seemed to be yet more pitfalls that prevented her from moving.

Behind her was a poster advertising a children's book: 'Little Peter wants to be a socialist. An illustrated book. 4.50 francs. On sale at the *Humanité* bookshop, 142 Rue Montmartre.'

Francine was correcting the proofs of an article. She didn't think it was worth raising her head to see who she was dealing with.

'What do you want?'

'M. Cachin advised me to ask for your help … I want to have a look at Lecointre's articles on squatting.'

She grumbled as she shuffled through the books full of cross-references before coming upon the one that contained the information I needed.

'January 1912 … Take this down … Yes. So January 1912, nearly every day … That was the beginning, Lecointre was covering the problem of housing in Paris, in general. It was perfect from every point of view, political, economic … February, August of the same year. Then January 1913 and July. After that, it went quiet. The newspapers are on your right, classified by year and by month. Try to leave them in their proper order…'

It was child's play to put together the epic story of Cochon's band.

The 'founding father' had spent three years in the African Battalion, the Af. Bat., the price he had to pay for being a conscientious objector, and he had created his 'Trade Union' after many different propaganda skirmishes of tenants against 'The Vultures', the nickname he gave to his sworn enemies, the property owners who took advantage of the housing crisis to hand-pick their future tenants.

His likeness was captured in a photo the size of a postage stamp accompanying an article by Lecointre: you could see his face half-covered by an incredible moustache which put Cachin's to shame, a Spanish hat with a large brim concealed his eyes. As a final touch, a black scarf rose out of the starched collar and tickled his chin.

The beginning of the rebellion against the landlords dated back to the eviction order passed against him and his family to be carried out on 31 December 1911… On the morning of New Year's Day, a hundred policemen, half on foot, half on horseback, couldn't get into 'Fort Cochon' as the occupied apartment had been named, as all the entrances had been barricaded with solid beams. The counter-attack was spontaneously organized: the balance of forces was tipped well in favour of the besieged by midday.

The passive resistance became more and more sophisticated: legal procedure was answered by swaggering humour. To save a street-trader, his wife and their eight children who were thrown on to the street, Cochon, himself a carpetmaker, and several comrades, carpenters, roofers, woodworkers, constructed a prefabricated house that they could erect, after practising for several days, in less than a quarter of an hour.

The fruit and vegetable seller stayed one night in the Jardin des Plantes, another in the courtyard of the National Assembly and in front of police headquarters!

One of Cochon's moments of glory was the one where he invaded the Salon de l'Habitat which was exhibiting several villas at the Grand Palais and gave them to families who had been evicted. On that occasion he had declared to Lecointre:

'They've made the houses and I've invented a way of using them!'

I scrutinized all the photos next without recognizing Francis Ménard. However the visit had not been in vain. I didn't know enough on the topic to give a scintillating lecture, but I could get by in conversation. As Irène said: 'I don't have to shine, I leave that to the stars.'

Before going I made sure that each paper was back in its proper place. I closed the door behind me, gently. Francine would never know to whom she had given this information.

CHAPTER 13

It was three o'clock in the afternoon before I decided to phone home. I had had lunch in a brasserie on the Rue Lafayette, a Lyon sausage downed with a generous quantity of Belgian beer. I was to spend the rest of the afternoon searching out all the public toilets: a large Kriek and I could out-stop the slowest bus route!

Irène picked up the phone before the end of the first ring.

'Hello, is that you?'

'Yes. I don't know if I'm coming home tonight. You seem worried . . . Has something happened?'

She answered me jokingly but I could sense the bravado in her tone.

'It sure has! You always disappear just when it's your turn to do the cooking . . . As if you were doing it on purpose . . . No, it's just that I'm really missing you at the moment.'

She said this last sentence so sadly that it was all I could do not to drop everything and hurry back to the Rue Maroc to console her.

'Just hang on for a little bit, Irène. You know I love you. I miss you a lot as well . . . It won't be long now. I don't understand much yet but my hunch is that the pieces of the jigsaw are fitting together . . . They're falling into place one by one but we won't know the outcome until we find the master key.'

'I'll wait. Anyway what else can I do! By the way, your colonel, Fantin, has tried several times to get hold of you. I didn't tell him you had an appointment at police headquarters. Was that right?'

'Yes. We're made for each other; your responses are exactly the same as mine. If he rings again, reassure him, I don't want him to panic. What does he want?'

'He wants to see you as soon as possible. Today if you can. What shall I tell him?'

I didn't see any need to enter into negotiations with Fantin again. In any case my time was already taken up for the rest of the day and a good part of the night. It would be impossible to fit in a journey from Paris to Aulnay and back without jeopardizing my plans.

'No, I won't have time. Put him off until tomorrow morning, even if it's quite early... But here's a thought: tell him to put himself out for once! I'm not budging any more. He could expect it when I was working for him... He tore up the contract, and the car service with it!'

'At what time?'

'Between eight and nine. Anyway I don't know why he's so worried, the press is sitting on the whole affair really thoroughly. There's not a word in the papers. It's a god-send: we can just quietly get on with it.'

Irène whispered her goodbyes.

'Big kiss... Don't be too late. Be careful.'

I settled my bill, my expression gloomy. I didn't like leaving her in such a state. The waiter got worried.

'You look like you've got the blues...'

I perked up and shook my head.

'No, in fact I'm just pulling myself together!'

Saying which I slipped out. A gang had surrounded the Double-Six, deprived kids in shabby clothes, their hair greased down. They scattered, leaving me room to reach the door. The boldest one, a puny little boy with missing teeth, a lick of yellow hair falling into his eyes, plucked up enough courage to stick his head inside.

'That's some car! Where's she from, mister?'

I winked at him.

'The other side of the Atlantic. From the USA.'

I had pronounced the initials with an American accent which I had learnt from Bob. The brat's eyes grew wide at the sound of the magic word. He withdrew, repeating to himself, 'You Essay... You Essay,' and disappeared, his head lost in the clouds, with the rest of the gang following him.

I went over every detail on the way. No room for mistakes, I was ready to confront Francis Ménard and his friends. By now, the sun was shining. I dropped down towards Concorde and went up the Avenue des Champs-Elysées at top speed, barely slowing down at the Place de l'Etoile for the rows of nostalgics who went to stand to attention under the Arc de Triomphe.

I reflected that I had never again needed to crook my arm that way, my fingers straining at my temple... As soon as I had been demobbed, my nervous system had quickly forgotten all those automatic gestures. They could get whole regiments of generals, admirals, field marshals to march past under my nose, my elbow wouldn't twitch...

Going round the monument I generously gave them an ironic salute just to prove they would never put one over on me again. A lump in my throat warned me that I shouldn't be so sure... Red, white and blue, Alsace, Lorraine, the Historic Enemy, we had had it stuffed down our throats from nursery school... It wasn't surprising that I should still feel something, one afternoon in January, on the road to Neuilly. A big surprise was waiting for me at the Rue Breteville: armed police had blocked off both ends of the street and were checking anyone who wanted to go through. I moved in without worrying: the car was a sufficient sign of my standing. I would just melt into the background as far as the police were concerned.

The reason for this show of force became apparent as I came level with number 77. The gate was covered with banners, slogans written on cardboard making public the demands of the squatters: 'Housing for the workers', 'No more evictions'.

I went fifty metres beyond the house to park the car where the taxi had stopped. I then went back on my tracks, on foot, with the disinterested air of a passer-by so as not to call attention to myself from the police. They were busy in the garden; some men who looked like workers were strengthening the barricades that had been put up in the parts that were least protected by the iron fence. Concentrating on their task they didn't see me and I made my presence known by rapping on a bar with my key. A guy in a cap with a large piece of black material wrapped round his waist turned around.

'Hey, you, what do you want?'

He approached with a heavy step, one shoulder after another plunging towards the ground, in rhythm with the opposite foot. He stopped at a respectable distance, leaning with his hands on a long club.

'Can I come in?'

'You don't look like someone who lives on the street... To look at you, you wouldn't think that you were sleeping rough!'

I waited till he'd finished making fun of me.

'I'm a journalist from *L'Humanité*. We're thinking of doing a feature on what's going on here...'

He had a change of attitude and he gestured to me to wait a while.

'Well, that's a different matter... Don't move, I'll go and find Pedro.'

The man with the rolling gait came back accompanied by an older man, maybe about fifty, small in stature, with his hair swept back. The thinness of his face was accentuated by a sparse beard trimmed round his chin. The newcomer's eyes glittered brilliantly in the deep sockets that cast a gloomy shadow over the upper part of his face. He was meticulously dressed, which made him look like a man with a small private income or a professor. He placed his hands on the top of the little wall, between two bars.

'So they tell me you're a reporter... That means the press has already got wind of our exploits! You're getting better, less than an hour behind the police...'

'They have more scouts.'

'Sometimes they're the same...'

He quickly modified his suggestion:

'I'm not referring to you... You don't look like a Trojan horse. But I harbour no illusions about your comrades in the tabloid press. Are you new to *L'Humanité*?... In any case I don't know many people there... The anarchists are no longer treated like gods there... We were given better treatment when Jaurès was in charge...'

Now was the time to put in my pitch and to pile on the conviction: the Open Sesame depended on my tongue.

'I've been working for a while on the rag. I was teamed up with Lecointre before the war... Not to follow Cochon's team, unfortunately... It's one of the biggest regrets of my professional life. I worked on the sports pages. Now I cover sports and society...'

I had noticed him react at the mention of Lecointre's name. My passport! Who would mention a journalist four years after his death except a real friend?

Pedro weighed up the pros and cons and suddenly made up his mind. He turned to the character with the club.

'OK Georges, take him in.'

It was enough to pull apart two hand-carts to free the main entrance. Soon I was within the defence system of those who had put themselves under siege. Pedro led me towards the building. Two enormous stone lions flanked the sweep of stairs which led to an entrance hall tiled in white marble. The walls were hidden by greenery, azaleas and exotic plants. A staircase with a ramp of polished iron running alongside and steps covered by a thick dark carpet led up to the floors above. Proletarian couples in working clothes were strolling through this extravagant luxury, studying the statues, the pictures, running their fingers over the surface to savour the size and the materials. A woman was changing a baby that she had laid down in a recess near a bouquet of roses signed Carolus-Duran. Pedro caught my look of stupefaction.

'That's what the revolution would be like, wouldn't it? Art and luxury for all... You weren't expecting that... be honest!'

'No, I have to admit I wasn't. They told us there was a house being squatted at Neuilly. They didn't say it was a palace... The owners won't go easy on you.'

He led me into a room where the walls were hung with red brocade.

'I've set up my office in here. Red everywhere! I couldn't find a black room... So then, you were working with Lecointre...'

'Yes, from time to time.'

'I think he copped it as well... Quite a few of our mates were killed and your employers are responsible. At least in a large part.'

I hadn't come all the way here to get involved in a heated argument about the treachery of the Socialist leaders in 1914 and their rallying to the nation.

'It's not clear-cut. Jaurès would not have hesitated to row against the current; in fact, he was the first Frenchman killed in that damned war. Very symbolic. We're not going to rewrite history this evening... What's important to me is my paper. You get more down to earth as you get older. Can I start asking you some questions?'

Pedro nodded his head.

'Go ahead.'

He sat in a magnificent antique chair, happy just at the idea that some king, Louis or Henri, could be used as a receptacle for his anarchist arse!

'OK. First question: are you trying to revive the "Tenants' Trade Union" with this action?'

'No, that's not on the agenda. We're not there yet. We're not yet as influential as before the war. When you add up those who died and the traitors, it mounts up. This manoeuvre is a trial run.

We're here almost by accident; Neuilly was never a particularly fruitful recruiting ground ... That's obvious!'

'So then why did you choose this place?'

'Like I said, it was chance. It fell into our hands without warning. A fantastic coming together of circumstances. With our numbers, we were up to taking over a hovel in the Goutte d'Or ... Not a single paper would have been interested in the event. A complete flop. On the other hand, an aristocrat's residence in the heart of Neuilly, two seconds from the Bois de Boulogne and its good-time girls, you're on a winner. The imagination runs wild. We're front page news! You'll find out somehow, some day so I might as well tell you straight away: this shack belongs to the Viscountess Salreille.'

I whistled with admiration. Her name turned up every week in the society columns alongside the likes of Rothschild, Meffray, Rochefoucauld or Broglie ...

'You're pushing it a bit! All those people have powerful connections with government ministers. They'll turf you out in no time ...'

Pedro shrugged his shoulders. The objection didn't go far.

'If it was as simple as that, the police would have got rid of us already. We're not running any risks at the moment, the occupation was initiated by the viscountess.'

He watched me closely to assess the effect of his words.

'... Takes your breath away, doesn't it!'

'It certainly does. I would have thought of everything except that as an explanation. What's her interest in organizing the invasion of her own home by a miserable band of men, women and children? Anarchists to cap it all ... It's complete madness!'

'Don't give yourself a headache; they're the ones with the funny ideas. A disappearing race: aristocrats with left-wing tendencies... There were a few during the Revolution. The Salreilles have been at it for a while, they were already supporting Cochon in secret before the war. Their own, very individual, way of giving to charity. They must have decided that we're more efficient than the local priest on the Avenue de Neuilly. At least the money they put our way can be used for shoes for our kids, instead of chamois leathers to polish up the pope's baubles...'

He spat to rinse out his mouth.

'Can I take notes and use some of this in my article?'

'I'm telling you these details to put some of the personalities in context... Before '14 they didn't want their role to be made public. They're showing their hand with this little turn. You're the journalist, you do your job... The viscountess is really involved: she's gone as far as having an estate built with ten villas to house evicted families. They're still there, in Romainville, Rue de l'Emancipation. With ridiculous rents; it's not the sort of thing that's going to change the world, but I don't see any reason to refuse gestures of goodwill just because they come from the opposition! We're doing them a small favour in return today: the Salreilles have built a mansion in the 16th district, near La Muette...'

'This one wasn't enough for them?'

'That's just the problem. This palace is rented. It belongs to a branch of the Vallombreuse family, I don't remember which one... The Salreilles wanted to move out within the next few weeks although their lease still has eighteen months to go. You would have thought the upper classes could have sorted things out among themselves. It seems not. Their landlord, blue-blooded though he is, is as tough as any slum landlord! If you ask me, it must be hard to put the screws on somebody rich enough to pay the rent on a pad like this. They hope to rake it in right up to the last moment. To cut a long story short, the Salreilles are sub-letting the palace to us, until such time as their landlord gives in. For us it's a windfall that enables us to relaunch the movement without any risks…'

He got up and stretched himself before continuing:

'…I'm very glad to be active again. We were beginning to get bored and rusty… Are you thirsty?'

I accepted the offer. Pedro led me to the kitchens where a chef in full kit was busying himself around his pots. A young girl dressed as a maid was peeling vegetables. Pedro introduced them to me.

'These are our comrades Paul and Yolande. The aristos have left them in our service as long as we're here. They had cold feet at first, what with all the stories told about us… Women in common and the world turned upside down. Now we know each other, things are easier. Isn't that so, Paul?'

'Yes, sir. Sir is quite right.'

My smile did not go unnoticed by Pedro. He wasn't fooled. 'Comrade' Paul had bent his head and agreed with the boss ever since his first pair of short pants. For him masters were as indispensable to the running of the world as the remains of the lobster were for his Sunday dinner. He certainly much preferred the class from which the Salreilles came. It was a question of culture: they shared the same one, each in their own way. He knew how long you had to cook a dish and they never made a mistake with the cutlery when it came to eating it. These anarchists, you were lucky if they remembered that forks existed! And they called themselves the future of the world…

CHAPTER 14

The young woman gave us coffee but they refused to have some with us. Just seeing us sitting down in their kitchen was beyond their comprehension. To confirm my credentials as a journalist, I went back to interviewing Pedro.

'Are you expecting to stay here long?'

'No, not in terms of years. The owner must have gone to the civil courts already... They'll allow an eviction, it's as plain as the nose on your face. The key is to hang on for three or four days to draw as many people as possible. The cops won't attack, the Vallombreuse family will come to a gentlemen's agreement out of court. We're not such good publicity for them.'

Insidiously, I slipped in my request.

'I'd like to follow the whole turn of events for twenty-four hours... I could write an article, hour by hour, a sort of living record. Do you think that's feasible?'

'Yeah, no problem, there's room for an army of journalists. Come and choose your room.'

I climbed the colossal staircase clinging on to the banister to avoid walking on the carpet. On the journey, and it really was a journey given how long the corridors were, I kept staring at all the people we came across.

The landing on the first floor was cluttered with suitcases, boxes, trunks, all the bric-à-brac of moving. Children of all ages were playing around it. In a drawing-room women on their knees on the white marble tiles were making up large banners out of old pieces of material. One of them was writing the letters in wax crayon while the second concentrated on going over the marks with black paint. A banner was drying near the fireplace, leaning on sculpted fireguards:

WORKERS WITH CHILDREN
ARE TREATED LIKE CRIMINALS:
DON'T HAVE ANY MORE CHILDREN

The letters of another slogan stretched over a mauve-covered sofa, following the line of the cushions and armrests:

GHT WORKERS' FAM ... 35 CHIL ... N

The second floor seemed to be less busy. A young couple were necking in the corner, crushed against each other. The woman's thick heavy hair coiled around her companion's neck. A violent wave of desire gripped me by the throat as I remembered my recent taxi ride ... The feel of her hair and of her hesitant tongue ...

In front of us, around a table with carved feet, three men were absorbed in reading books bound in real leather taken from a library whose shelves covered a large part of the wall. Pedro showed me an enormous room where the walls were hung with pink paper.

'Here, this is the lady's chamber. D'you like it? ... It's all one shade, the sheets, the furniture, the curtains, the lamps. Makes you feel you're in someone's sugar-bowl!'

I was about to enter my cocoon when the door of the neighbouring room opened. I recognized his profile at once. Francis Ménard alias Sorinet alias Goyon. Pedro held out his hand and greeted him.

'So, there you are, you're in good shape! You've slept for at least a week...' (He turned to me and pointed at me with his finger.) 'I hope you don't mind, I've given you a journalist from *L'Humanité* as a neighbour... In times of war...'

I thought about Pedro's last words in silence, imagining how they might sound to a guy wanted for desertion. Pedro introduced Ménard to me.

'Marcel Migeon, one of our leading cadres. Perhaps you've heard of him?'

I shook my head in the negative. Migeon had been in the file of anarchists who had disappeared in the war that I had looked through at police headquarters. He would go through the whole list if he stayed on the run. Then he could go on to take the names off the monuments to the dead or even better off the wooden crosses in the military cemeteries. Three names in less than a month, without counting the real one... He changed them more frequently than an American star!

Francis Ménard was even more striking when you saw him close up: there wasn't a centimetre of his skin still in one piece. Hundreds of fine scars criss-crossed his cheeks, his nose, his forehead. A slightly deeper cut pulled his right eye to one side and gave him a nervous tic, like something twinkling. I didn't recall any wounds like this. It didn't look like anything I knew, not even the injuries received from the first grenades, the 'hair-brush' ones, a wooden handle with the explosive tied on to a kind of plate with a piece of wire... They killed as many of the people throwing them as they did Germans. We should have given them our stockpile right at the beginning!

He must surely have had a bomb explode between his hands, some gadget stuffed full of shot... Ménard put an end to the scrutiny by moving towards the staircase.

'Is he in charge of this operation?'

'No, each has their own section. I'm responsible for things in Neuilly, in permanent direct contact with the Salreilles. Marcel is in charge of something quite different... It'll make even more noise than our little game!'

I barely succeeded in holding back my desire to shower him with questions, to grab him by the collar if he didn't answer fast enough.

I spoke slowly, my jaws tense.

'You're getting ready for another squat? Where?'

'No, we like to vary our pleasures. He's working on an article, a bit like you. This is the journalists' hidey-hole... I don't know what yours will be like, but his is already an absolute bombshell. As powerful as Zola's 'J'accuse'. Well nearly...'

Everything was falling into place perfectly; the papers that Fantin coveted so much were there, at that precise moment, only five metres away on a table in exotic wood or in the drawer of a desk made of exquisite marquetry. With no guards... If you didn't count the passionate readers, Pedro and the guy that you could hear breathing heavily in the corner. It would be better to wait for the right moment. I took up my role of reporter again.

'When does he intend to publish it, this article of his?'

'Not for another three or four days. We'll take advantage of the stir caused by the stories of the "populist-aristocrats". You'll see. Keep in touch, I can't say any more than that... In any case it won't be an exclusive for *L'Humanité* despite all the sympathy I still have for Lecointre's friends. We'll bring out a newspaper for the occasion, one solitary number: *Le Canard noir*.

Pedro left me to settle into the pink room. If it had only been the colour; but everything, the material, the hangings, the bed-linen was also impregnated with a heavy perfume. I opened the window on to the garden. Down below, I could make out the silhouette of Georges, my 'concierge', busy lighting a fire of wooden planks. Mounting the guard was turning into a freezing cold job. As for myself, my plans sorted themselves out: relaxation into the pink satin and mulling things over.

With a flutter of wings the Muse could have taken me for a languid nymph!

I propped myself up to take stock of myself in a mirror leaning at an angle above a small dressing-table... Rather it would have to be a large beating of wings! She would have to be blind drunk, my Muse!

They sent a boy up at about eight o'clock to call me for supper. I was on the second sitting, the kids had eaten first.

Paul and Yolande, the comrade cooks, had really done their bit. Oysters from Belon to start, cold cuts from Daburon to follow, shoulder of mutton, beans, cheese, sorbet, wine from Chablis and Pommard. The front pages of the papers debated the necessity of bringing back bread rationing.

Anarchy has its virtues.

Francis Ménard was eating three seats down from me. He was drinking heavily and I was sorry not to have him next to me to help him along. I melted away when one of the readers from the second floor began to hum the first notes of the revolutionary repertoire. *A cappella*...

Be warned, be warned,
The Revolution is coming,
Be warned,
The Young Guard is filling the streets,
Death to all priests.

Several children were still running around the flames in the garden, spellbound by their gigantic shadows, thrown up on to the stone façade. On the first floor, in the room where they had been making banners, men and women were putting down mattresses and blankets on the floor, a sort of makeshift camp set amongst the trappings of an imperial court: this was the children's dormitory. A tall bearded man with gangling limbs was rocking a baby to the rhythm of the song which came up from the dining-room, marking the verses with a kiss on the baby's forehead:

Death to all priests.

Silence descended at one o'clock in the morning after a group of five or six men had crossed the threshold. Reinforcements. They stocked up with blankets and left the building again to take up guard-duty near the fire. Ménard had gone up to his room just after midnight. Alone. I heard him pace up and down, then sit down to write. Waves of silence interspersed with furious pacing. He worked until two o'clock before going to sleep.

The watch was focused on the outside, the gates, but it was useless to try anything for the time being. I was no match for fifteen sturdy, determined men.

I passed the time by stripping down my automatic, an

11.66mm Webley. I spread out the parts and the rounds on the eiderdown. Counting the seconds I closed my eyes and reassembled it. One, two, three ... at a hundred and ten, with the gun still unloaded, I tested the firing mechanism a couple of times, without pulling back the breech-block, the only way of making sure all the parts were back in place, a hundred and twelve, using the tips of my fingers, I put the rounds into the clip, and slotted it in, a hundred and thirty-five I pulled back the hammer behind the slide to the half-way position, lightly held back by my thumb ... I opened my eyes at a hundred and forty.

In the trenches, you had to take less than two minutes to impress ... Lack of practice.

The next time I wouldn't count so fast!

A quartet of insomniacs were pushing back the limits of fatigue as they discussed the relative merits of Bakunin, Louise Michel and Malatesta. I tried to follow the conversation for a while. At three o'clock the conversation petered out in yawns and mumbled words when one of the bearded men, whose voice sounded like the one who was singing at the end of the meal, threw in the name of Kropotkin.

'And Kropotkin, do you think it's behaving like an anarchist to settle down in Moscow, well in Dimitrov, I won't spoil the argument for the sake of a few kilometres ... He's supporting a regime that's putting our brothers in prison.'

They were off for another round. Everything was dragged in: the Polish uprising in 1863, theories about the ice age, the escape from the Peter and Paul fortress in 1876, the collaboration with Elisée Reclus. I was standing with my ear glued to the door, the only position that would keep me awake.

They took about an hour to liquidate Kropotkin alias Lavachov and the man with the beard refrained from starting on another track. I waited a moment before daring to go out into the corridor. Nothing moved. I crept to Francis Ménard's door, my piece in my left hand hidden behind the lapels of my jacket. The man of many names felt very safe as he hadn't bothered to turn the key in the lock. The door opened with a squeak even though I'd taken care to lean on the handle to soften the movement of the hinges. Ménard turned over in his bed, his sleep disturbed. I moved towards him with the greatest care, having made sure the door closed silently this time.

I held my breath as I walked, my muscles straining, on tiptoe. I had known the life of a hunted man, for months on end, in one hole or another ten metres from the German lines ... The fact that one slept was the hardest to credit. Not for long: two, three minutes. The slightest noise, a breath of wind, a rat worrying at a bit of flesh would get you on your feet quicker than an electric shock. Even when you were on leave, you couldn't get out of the habit. You would find yourself panicking, looking for your gun, at two in the morning in a hotel room with a girl who thought you had gone mad ...

It was a question of life and death.

Ménard must have been warned by some sixth sense, as if the shock waves of my movement made contact with his defences. He sat up in bed with his eyes wide open with fear and stared straight at the spot where I stood. I anticipated his reactions and before he could shout I leapt on him striking with the butt of my gun. The blow landed just above the temple. He fell back on the pillow without a sound.

The toffs furnished their rooms on the same principle but

varying the colours: here the dominant colour was green, you felt as if you were living in the middle of a lettuce. Only a desk in lacquered wood jarred with the rest of the furnishings. It was easy to deduce that it was something introduced by Ménard. It had been brought at his request, for his writing. The keys to the flap were in a pocket of his trousers, on the back of the chair. I took everything to be seen on the shelves, without looking through it, leaving only the pen and ink.

I was still busy distributing documents around the various pockets of my clothes when there were two soft knocks at the door. I hid in the corner behind the cupboard. A shape appeared in the doorway...

'Hey, Marcel...'

Pedro's voice. I swallowed and my saliva going past my Adam's apple echoed to my ears as loudly as a sink that's just been unblocked. Pedro called again without any better result. And for a good reason! He turned towards a second man whose shadow could be made out on the ground.

'The guy's still sleeping! It's true he must be worn out after having been on the go without stopping for three days... It doesn't matter, we can talk about it tomorrow morning.'

Pedro closed the door again; the sound of their footsteps went off away from the staircase. They were going back to their rooms. Before I left I gagged Ménard and tied his wrists securely to the bed-head. I took care to draw the pale green sheets around him without making a joke out of it and tucking him in...

One solitary man was on guard-duty, down in the garden. The others were sleeping around braziers, wrapped up in blankets, their sticks within arm's reach. It wasn't worth trying;

any attempt on my part to get through the gates would have attracted their suspicion. I found a hide-out, mindful of the comings and goings of the man on watch. The house began to come alive with the babies' first cries, at about six o'clock. The ideal moment to fade away.

I didn't come across anyone except a man half stupefied with lack of sleep, who was going to the toilet and, on the staircase, two women lightly clothed who were coming up from the kitchens carefully holding saucepans full of hot water in which the babies' bottles were heating up.

I turned around to have a better look at their bodies in movement. I was gripped by the cold as soon as I set foot on the stairs. Georges nabbed me half-way between the pair of seated lions and the gates, punctuating his 'Good morning, comrade!' with a loud yawn accompanied by a long-drawn-out stretch.

'Not warm, eh... Have you come to keep me company? There's not one that can match me half-way: they're all snoring! Even the reinforcements that came last night... Everything OK?'

'Not too bad, I'll sleep better tonight... I'll go and get the papers to see if there's any coverage yet. You can open up for me, I know a kiosk that opens early, not far from Sablons.'

Georges set to pushing the barricades away without asking any questions, after he had made sure the street was empty.

'Oh you reporters, you're all the same. Those damned rags are a real drug... The cops aren't here yet, but don't take long coming back, they're likely to block everything off this time.'

He held me back as I was leaving:

'If you go past a tobacconist, bring me back a packet of Disque Bleu. I don't like always cadging off friends...'

One of the men huddled round the fire had got up, dragged out of sleep by the commotion, Georges reassured him as he pulled out the last hand-cart that was blocking the gate.

'It's the newspaper guy, the one we were talking about last night... He's going to get papers and some tobacco... There's no danger, there's not a helmet to be seen in the area.'

The newcomer turned back to his spot but his gaze caught mine for a split second. The light from the flames distorted his features, deepening the shadows or smoothing out the structures. I looked at him intently, searching unsuccessfully through my memory for his name or the last time we had met. The hesitation he showed as he went back to his sleeping spot revealed that he was going through the same mental search. With the same result.

I got back to the Packard. No one had touched it. I sped off to the Rue Maroc with the unpleasant sensation of marking a trail with the wheels of the car. His name was on the tip of my tongue, I couldn't stop him dancing in my thoughts, like a puppet...

As for Georges, he could kiss goodbye to his packet of cigs.

I stopped at the Café des Travailleurs to buy the paper. An old habit.

CHAPTER 15

Irène was still asleep, her face buried in the pillow. I stretched out beside her, still dressed, in the warm aura of her body, waiting for her to wake up.

The long night must have had its effect on me for I woke out of a dream with a start as she scraped the ashes in the stove with the poker.

'Oh shit! I fell asleep... What time is it?'

'You needed it... Stay in bed, I'll make some coffee. It's nearly eight o'clock. I would have woken you anyway, Fantin is due within the hour... So, have you got something new?'

I pointed at my jacket draped over a chair, at the foot of the bed.

'I think so. I nabbed the ghost from Roissy-en-France, an anarchist who passes under a bunch of false names. Francis Ménard, in fact. In a mansion in Neuilly... Anyway, I'll explain it all to you later, it's a bit complicated. The main thing is that I picked up a pile of papers that he was about to go public with. Including those of the blackmailer, the bloke they found dead at his villa in Villepinte... Take them out, there are some in every pocket.'

She brought them over. The first ones were a series of scattered notes and different attempts to start the one article.

Ménard was trying to work out his line of argument. Fantin's name cropped up every two lines ... Ménard was trying to rewrite in the language of the militant the crucial document: a long carefully penned letter in violet ink, signed Julien Versois. At first glance I could see that there were two parts: first an introduction about ten lines long written in very upright characters, then a long text in the same hand but this time with the letters sloping along the line, as if the writer wanted to recreate two different voices. I propped myself up on the pillows.

> The following text was written under the author's dictation on the 21st November 1919 at the sanatorium of Villepinte in my sole presence. The signature on the bottom of the document is that of Julien Versois who was brought back on the 12th July 1917 from the surgical unit of the Fismes campaign and who died on ...'

The date of death was written in black. The writer must have left a space, like a form, while the man whose story followed was still alive.

> '... 22nd November 1919. To forestall all doubts as to its authenticity, Julien Versois has also marked the bottom of the letter with his right index finger.'
>
> Roger Fauge, nurse at Villepinte.

> *Before my departure, I want to cleanse my conscience absolutely of the worst act of cowardice that I have ever committed. Yet I have collected a heavy burden of such acts in my life, as has all the world, I should imagine. But it*

would be very sad if we had to carry all this weight. I have kept quiet until now, because it would have been useless to go back over things; those still alive, the survivors, would have to come to terms with their memories, is what I thought to myself… But when you know that you're about to go over to the other side and that the hereafter goes on for a bloody long time… I'm not kidding myself, I know it's going to happen soon, so if I'm going to meet him, I don't want to be ashamed of myself. I want to reveal everything about the death of a man that I am about to meet again.

The events took place in June '17, just after the major offensives, we were holding the line above Reims, between Courcy and Loivre. Our target was a hamlet at the point of a triangle, Brimont. But the Jerries had managed to dig themselves in down the slope, out of sight of our observation balloons. We took advantage of the rare moments of calm, when they were letting their cannon cool down, to shore up our shelters. They kept telling us that they were at the end of their tether and we were damned surprised when they attacked in full daylight, on the morning of the 16th, without any preparatory artillery fire. I was in a shell crater, with this poor guy, Daniel Sorinet… We soon realized that we wouldn't be able to hold out. Everywhere we were retreating in disorder… They took back a good kilometre of ground during that morning… As soon as they set up their guns, the deluge started again. It was hell. The second assault was even worse; they were madmen… We had crossed the National 44 by noon… That wasn't allowed! That symbol was vital to the generals: you can imagine, a nice straight line, it looks good in the papers... They sent the NCOs down the new front line to bawl us out or raise our morale, we weren't quite sure which... Our sector had inherited the top brass, Colonel Fantin de Larsaudière. In three years of campaigning that must have been the first time he was within gunshot of the enemy... He was among that bunch of officers that kept up with the movements of the enemy's large artillery pieces so that they could set up their command posts well out of reach. It wasn't surprising the orders always arrived too late: they had to come from so far away! Anyway, it was one hell of a baptism; their artillery was flattening the hills. On top of that, the missiles were fucking up... like damp squibs. Sorinet was listening out for them; he could tell just by the sound of the impact, the calibre of a shell... There was a continuous stream of faulty shells. Sometimes you get that, a bad lot... Fucking hell! I was the first to get a whiff; a disgusting musty smell, something sickly... I screamed for the last time in my life: 'Gas! They're throwing gas bombs!' We rushed towards the masks but a bit of wind blew a gust smack in my face just as I got tangled in the straps. I tried to hold my breath until my lungs were bursting but those shitty straps wouldn't hold... The most I could do was to just place it over my face... That wasn't good enough, I inhaled a dose of poison. I was badly burnt internally. My eyes were streaming, I was vomiting continuously without letting go of the mask and I fell to the bottom of the trench half dead but still lucid.

The Germans would soon come and do a clean sweep, bayonets at the ready... We did the same thing, no quarter given... At a time like this, the only way to avoid having your throat cut in your rat-hole was to mount a counter-attack, with hand to hand fighting. Instead of climbing on to the parapet Colonel Fantin was standing in the shelter, frozen still, his flare gun by his side. Sorinet had come up to him, he was shaking him by the shoulders, holding him by the sort of decorations stuck on their chests… 'Tell them to move otherwise we're all done for! They're not going to do us any favours… For Christ's sake, they're waiting for the signal!'

The voices came to me distorted by the mask. All the rest of the section were scattered along the line for about fifty metres, at the bottom of shell craters, their eyes glued to the peak, ready to climb up and fight for their lives when the signal to counter-attack came…

It was the other companies that rescued us from the slaughter when they pushed back the waves of cleaners-up in the trenches. Sorinet was still holding on to Fantin: 'You fucker, you nearly killed us all, shit-head.' There was fighting all around us, with me lying on the ground and the trench falling in on me without my being able to move… Finally Sorinet's shower of curses pulled Fantin out of his stupor. He had realized what those few minutes of cowardice could have cost him. As if in a dream I saw him drawing his regulation pistol and aiming at Sorinet at close quarters… He thought I was dead, it's true I was already half-buried! Finally he knelt at my side, he was fumbling at my belt, I asked myself why. I understood when I felt my trousers slipping down my legs and the breeze on my bare skin… I let it all happen, unable to lift a finger. He had taken off his own and thrown them over me before dressing himself again. And yet they were old rags that I'd been wearing for the last six months in the mud of Champagne... But at least they weren't full of shit like his!

That's right, the colonel had stood there shitting himself, like a kid!

Nobody asked any questions when, later on, Fantin explained that he had had to execute the soldier Sorinet who was fleeing from his post after refusing to mount the assault after the Germans attacked. The military police completed the weighty file on Daniel Sorinet the anarchist with the words: 'Desertion in the face of the enemy. Exemplary execution on the 16th June 1917.'

That squared everything and fitted into the way things were. I was picked up two hours later covered in my vomit and his shit. I was transferred to Fismes, a hospital behind the lines and then here, to Villepinte. Two and a half years of agony for one breath too many and a bloody tangled strap...

The document finished with Julien Versois's signature and a print of his right index finger.

I stayed for a long minute staring at the papers, my mind a blank. I held them out to Irène.

'Read that and you'll get the picture!'

She read the words in silence, giving a nervous shake of her head at the more horrible passages. By the time she reached the last sentences she was wiped out.

'It's not possible, what scum! Now I understand why it was so important to him that you shouldn't know what was in the document. He had to get it back at all costs … His wife sleeping with other people, that was just a bit of smoke to cloud your eyes! Do you think she was part of all this?'

I had used the time that Irène had spent reading Julien Versois's letter to make a start on piecing together the story.

'Yes and no … What's for sure is that they both tried to bamboozle me. Then the colonel played his own hand. It wasn't in their interests that this shameful episode should be made public: Fantin, the colonel of the regiment with the most medals in France, you can see the picture! Nor for the Cognacs de Larsaudière ex-Darsac … It would have been certain ruin … The nurse at Villepinte had acted cunningly even if he wasn't a professional. He started off by sending proof of what he had without revealing his identity … That way he could judge how much Fantin was willing to pay for his silence. First step. Then he realized the full scope of the possibilities that were open to him: no more or less than the Darsac fortune. He had them by the throat. Fantin realized what was happening and realized that he couldn't handle it on his own. It was no good calling the police in, the cops would probably open up the whole can of worms by mistake. That must have been where Bob came in. The colonel's wife rubbed shoulders with speculators and she had made some juicy profits out of war stock like the tins of pig meat. As if by chance, Bob was hanging around the area … As soon as there's a bit of money to be made … He recommended my services to the colonel, no hard feelings, for a few readies. He must have given him a spiel about American private eyes. So then Fantin must have set things up in cahoots with his wife. I think she'd been carrying on for donkey's years without it giving any grief, he probably had his own bits on the side … He played the role of the husband held up to ridicule, a blackmailer's victim to get me to reveal the tactless lover. In fact, I stirred up a hornet's nest ... The nurse understood pretty quickly that the net was getting tighter when I first went down to the sanatorium ...'

Irène interrupted me:

'Don't you think you're reading too much into it? You turned up at the sanatorium to meet Fantin's old batman, after his daughter attempted suicide ...'

'Yeah, well, exactly ... It's true that if there hadn't been that suicide attempt I would never have set foot in Villepinte. But Luce tried to kill herself when she found out about the ties between her mother and Emmanuel Alizan. Because of photos and letters that had been carelessly slipped into her handbag! A bit hard to swallow with hindsight, don't you think?'

She looked at me, aghast.

'Do you mean to say that her mother, knowingly, risked her daughter's life?'

'No, not her, but the colonel, it's a dead cert. It really confirmed all the descriptions he'd given me of his wife. From that moment my guard slipped, I just followed the scent like a little puppy ... Sure there was the story about the laudanum; the doctor hadn't prescribed it and Fantin made out he had. I filed that somewhere in my memory ... After a few days, Roger Fauge, the nurse, took fright. He wanted to cash in on the confession which fell into his hands by pure chance, just because he was on duty with a dying man. A unique opportunity to win huge sums of money but not at the risk of losing his life! He felt taken over by events. He had no choice: to stop Fantin he would have had to reveal the contents of the letter, thereby preventing himself from making a profit ... That's why he sent the demand for a meeting which I intercepted, in the hope of negotiating as quickly as possible. Fantin had reached his first goal…'

'Why, did he have another one?'

I kissed her on the forehead.

'Sure, the one that you sniffed out right from the start; to get rid of his wife in order to lay hands on the Darsac empire! By agreeing to play the part of a nymphomaniac for me she didn't realize that she was giving her husband a trump card. Maybe she had a hint of it at her daughter's failed suicide. We'll never know. As soon as the nurse showed himself, it was essential to get rid of me and to sort out how things would go at the meeting in Roissy-en-France. If you work it out, what Fantin expected to do was to wipe out the nurse and his wife under cover of an exchange of fire during an attempt at blackmail. He would have had no hesitation afterwards in using me as a witness that his wife was an out-and-out slut who could pleasure herself with a whole flight command! And I would have fallen into it…. Unluckily for him, the best laid plans often conceal a hidden trap. The weak spot was Francis Ménard…'

'Yeah, I still don't understand what the fuck he's doing in all this!'

'It's easy: he was teamed up with Daniel Sorinet, before the war. A little group of anarchists involved in the business of taking over flats, demonstrations where cops got done over…On the 11th November '18, when he did the rounds of his friends, it didn't take him too long…Practically the whole group was wiped out. He wanted to know how his mates had died and he came across "Desertion in face of the enemy. Exemplary execution." He set off on Fantin's trail and didn't let him go for an instant after that. It turned out to be well worthwhile.

When he followed him to Roissy-en-France he arrived in the middle of the bargaining. He didn't understand any more than I did but he jumped in without any hesitation when Fantin killed his wife and shot Roger Fauge. The colonel was the main threat so he knocked him out, taking advantage of the element of surprise. The nurse was only wounded, he seized his chance and fled with the documents and the money. Francis Ménard pursued him in his Carden. As for me I followed the convoy, lagging a bit behind, the time it took me to get out from behind the bus shelter... It was all over at Villepinte: Ménard had killed Roger Fauge when the nurse threatened him with a gun. The money was everywhere, on the ground, on the bed, covered in blood... The papers had gone...'

I got up and walked over to the kitchen to get out the bottle of bourbon. I poured some into a mug, to the halfway mark and tipped a glass of boiling water, which was meant for the coffee, over the alcohol. Irène passed me the sugar.

'The colonel is going to arrive at any minute... What have we decided? Shall we throw everything at him?'

I took a long swallow waiting for the grog to warm my innards before replying.

'Out of the question. We'll give all these papers back to Ménard. Let them publish it...'

It was all clear in my head. I wasn't doing it to get my revenge on all those fucking officers who sent us to our deaths a hundred times a day, while they warmed their arses in the pillboxes behind. Nor for Sorinet. He didn't give a monkey's about retaliation where he was.

Not even to crush Fantin... If you began to set yourself up in judgement in the midst of this butchery, you'd have to decimate all the commanding officers, from the subaltern to the five-star general and that was a lot of people!

No, without really admitting it to myself, it was only for an image in my mind: the toy collection in Luce's bedroom, the soft toys, the dolls' cots, the pretend dinner sets ... The feeling that we had no right to betray the dreams of childhood even if it was only a secret love for a pretty boy who was looking for promotion among the petticoats of officers' wives.

Mechanically I unfolded *Le Matin*. The rag announced the election of Deschanel to the Presidency of the Republic. When I picked up my bowl again, my fingers left inky prints.

CHAPTER 16

I swallowed the last mouthful of grog and the sugary dregs tasting of alcohol.

'I can tell these revelations are going to make a big stink... How would you like a week or two in the country?'

'Why, do you want to go?'

'It would be safer. With all the nutters who see themselves as the brothers of the Unknown Soldier and who dream about nothing but taking revenge, I would rather be cautious... I know the ideal spot, by the seaside in the south... We won't be able to swim yet but it'll be better than here...'

Irène agreed.

'OK. Count me in! Will you help me get the suitcases ready?'

I should have had a big clean-up at the sink... Heat the water, dry my hair... There was no time, Fantin would have had to hand me my dressing-gown. I could see to all that this evening. Allowing for a detour to Neuilly to give back the papers and the drive down Route 7, we could pack in six hours of driving before nightfall. I could probably have a long soak near Moulins or Roanne, depending on the traffic.

I filled the suitcases carelessly, emptying the drawers and shelves of the wardrobe. Ten minutes later we were on the landing; I turned the key in the lock.

Irène had slipped Julien Versois's confession into her handbag and she held it clutched to her bosom, her fingers splayed wide over the leather. I managed to take the luggage down in one trip and she held the boot open while I wedged the suitcases in between the jerry-cans of petrol.

The Packard barely vibrated when I turned the starter. I could see the engine was ticking over by the cloud of blue smoke coming from the rear. Irène was already wedged into her seat and was tucking a blanket over her legs to keep her from the cold. I joined her and was just easing off the handbrake when I noticed a powerful motor speeding down the Rue Tanger. Straight away I recognized Colonel Fantin's Vauxhall.

'Shit, there he is! Hang on tight, I'm going to shake him off...'

I stamped hard on the accelerator; the twelve cylinders sprang into action at once, from cold, and the Packard shot off with a scream of tyres. Fantin was thrown for a minute, then took up the chase. I had barely covered a few hundred metres in the direction of Boulevard de la Villette when a little black car cut in front of me. A Carden... They had taken the roof off, despite the cold, to be able to get four people in. In the rear I recognized Georges and the man who had held my glance a few hours before, at Neuilly. Irène hung on to my arm.

'They're mad! We're going to crash into them...'

Then she pointed out the blond boy to me:

'Look, that's the guy who was chatting me up to get me to learn Esperanto... You know, Dahvof...'

Now I remembered. We'd met at my own home! I had found him with Irène, one evening when I came back from Aulnay... He hadn't been able to place me this morning, when he was barely awake. It must have come back to him when they found Ménard tied to his bed.

I slammed on the brakes, at the same time turning the wheel. The Double-Six left the road sideways on, the wheels scraping on the pavement before coming to a halt.

I shot out of the car yelling:

'Hang on guys … I'll explain everything …'

They didn't want to hear; Pedro had stood up to take the pin out of the grenade. His hands separated and his arm traced out a semicircle against the sky in a rallying gesture. The grenade landed full-force against the wind-screen and exploded. The blast knocked me to the ground.

'Irène … Come with me … I love you …'

I managed to get up in spite of the agonizing pain that was spreading along my right arm. She hadn't had time to make the slightest movement, her fingers still gripped around her bag. And it was when I tried to take it from her that I realized that there was nothing but pain where my arm had been.

As soon as he saw the Carden cutting in front of Griffon's car, Fantin had drawn up by the pavement to see how events would unfold. Without moving, he watched the detective's desperate efforts to get Irène out of the burning chassis. When the fuel tank finally exploded, showering bits of twisted metal all round the front of the building, his only reaction was a shiver brought on by the wave of heat from the blaze.

The Carden and its four occupants fled towards the Rue Bello. The Colonel's Vauxhall did a half-turn and sped off towards Aulnay.

Inspector Aubry was quickly briefed. He came down to the site of the murder. The bodies of René and Irène were unrecognizable; the charred fingers of the young woman still held shreds of leather. The team from the laboratory managed to dig out a bit of the right rear tyre, it was all the firemen from the Quai de l'Oise managed to rescue from the flames. The track exactly matched the traces found at Roissy-en-France after the tragic meeting which cost Mme Fantin her life.

The press made it known as with one voice that a pair of private detectives were responsible for that killing as well as that of Roger Fauge, the nurse from Villepinte. Everything seemed to point to the fact that the detectives, taken on to deal with a blackmailer, had thought they had cards of their own to play. The journalists blamed the carnage in the Rue du Maroc on a mysterious rival gang which was never tracked down.

A few pages further on you could read the following announcement:

Sunday 18th January 1920 at 11:30
INAUGURATION
OF THE MEMORIAL MONUMENT
OF COURVILLIERS
(Statue by M. Armand Cuellard,
Grand Prix de Rome)
by M. Joseph Colleton, mayor of Courvilliers
In the presence of the honourable
Colonel Fantin de Larsaudière
of the heroic 296th Regiment.
Patriotic concert
given by the Invalids' Brass Band

MELVILLE INTERNATIONAL CRIME

Kismet
Jakob Arjouni
978-1-935554-23-3

Happy Birthday, Turk!
Jakob Arjouni
978-1-935554-20-2

More Beer
Jakob Arjouni
978-1-935554-43-1

One Man, One Murder
Jakob Arjouni
978-1-935554-54-7

The Craigslist Murders
Brenda Cullerton
978-1-61219-019-8

Death and the Penguin
Andrey Kurkov
978-1-935554-55-4

Penguin Lost
Andrey Kurkov
978-1-935554-56-1

The Case of the General's Thumb
Andrey Kurkov
978-1-61219-060-0

Nairobi Heat
Mukoma Wa Ngugi
978-1-935554-64-6

Cut Throat Dog
Joshua Sobol
978-1-935554-21-9

Brenner and God
Wolf Haas
978-1-61219-113-3

The Bone Man
Wolf Haas
978-1-61219-169-0

Murder in Memoriam
Didier Daeninckx
978-1-61219-146-1

A Very Profitable War
Didier Daeninckx
978-1-61219-184-3

He Died with His Eyes Open
Derek Raymond
978-1-935554-57-8

The Devil's Home on Leave
Derek Raymond
978-1-935554-58-5

How the Dead Live
Derek Raymond
978-1-935554-59-2

I Was Dora Suarez
Derek Raymond
978-1-935554-60-8

Dead Man Upright
Derek Raymond
978-1-61219-062-4

The Angst-Ridden Executive
Manuel Vázquez Montalbán
978-1-61219-038-9

Murder in the Central Committee
Manuel Vázquez Montalbán
978-1-61219-036-5

The Buenos Aires Quintet
Manuel Vázquez Montalbán
978-1-61219-034-1

Off Side
Manuel Vázquez Montalbán
978-1-61219-115-7

Southern Seas
Manuel Vázquez Montalbán
978-1-61219-117-1

Tattoo
Manuel Vázquez Montalbán
978-1-61219-208-6

Death in Breslau
Marek Krajewski
978-1-61219-164-5

The End of the World in Breslau
Marek Krajewski
978-1-61219-177-5

The Accidental Pallbearer
Frank Lentricchia
978-1-61219-171-3